SEASON OF THE WITCH

MARIAH FREDERICKS

schwartz & wade books · new york

Visit us on the Web! randomhouse.com/teens

Educators and librarians, for a variety of teaching tools, visit us at RHTeachersLibrarians.com

Library of Congress Cataloging-in-Publication Data
Fredericks, Mariah.
Season of the witch/Mariah Fredericks.—1st edition.
p. cm.
Summary: "A girl who is bullied experiments with witchcraft in order to get revenge on her attackers"—Provided by publisher.
ISBN 978-0-449-81277-8 (hc) — ISBN 978-0-449-81278-5 (lib. bdg.) — ISBN 978-0-449-81279-2 (ebook)
[1. Bullying—Fiction. 2. Witchcraft—Fiction. 3. Revenge—Fiction. 4. High schools—Fiction. 5. Schools—Fiction.] I. Title.
PZ7.F872295Se 2013
[Fic]—dc23
2012040028

The text of this book is set in 11.5-point Paradigm.

Book design by Rachael Cole

Printed in the United States of America

10 9 8 7 6 5 4 3 2 1

First Edition

This one is for Kristen—
"Thunderbolt and
lightning—
very, very frightening me."

YOU KNOW HOW IT IS *with little girls. It's all about the princesses. Cinderella, Sleeping Beauty, Ariel—gorgeous cartoon females yearning for their princes and trapped by jealous old witches. When I was a kid, me and my two best friends, Francesca and Elodie, had a princess club. Every day at school, we'd get together at recess and do the princess thing. The rules were strict: You could not be a princess if you didn't wear a dress to school that day. You could not be a princess unless you had something pink on your person—socks, hair band, whatever. And you had to have a favorite. In case you care, mine was Snow White. I was wild for that black hair–red lips combo.*

However, it was understood that you played a princess who had the same color hair as you. Francesca had blond hair, so she could do Cinderella and Sleeping Beauty. Elodie had red hair, perfect for Ariel. I had dark brown hair, which meant I was stuck with Belle from Beauty and the Beast. No one ever wanted to play the Beast, so we didn't do a lot of Belle stories.

We couldn't do Snow White either, no matter how much I begged.

Francesca said Snow White was too scary for her. So, for one reason or another, I never got to do my story.

When we played Cinderella, I was the stepmother and Elodie was the fairy godmother. We did Little Mermaid. Francesca was the made-up part of Flounder's sister, Goldie, and I was Ursula. Once I said we had to do Mulan, but Francesca and Elodie got bored with it because she wasn't really a princess and there was only one girl part. Also, she cut off her hair, which was a big fat no-no.

And that's how it was. Day after day, we would meet by the old iron bench under the tree in the recess yard. While the rest of the kids were climbing and swinging and chasing each other, Francesca and Elodie would sigh and dream and pretend to talk to woodland creatures—while I got stuck playing whatever lousy role they gave me.

And what I started wondering was, why did they get to decide? Who put them in charge?

One day, we were on the playground. Our teacher, Ms. Tina, was standing by the door, keeping an eye on the boys in case they started shoving. Francesca and Elodie were sitting on the little bench, trying to decide whether we would do the scene where Cinderella's stepmother says she can't go to the ball or the one where the fairy godmother turns the pumpkin into a coach. I stood to one side, waiting to hear if I was a stepsister, one of the mice, or what.

And that's when I said "I'm tired of Cinderella."

Francesca and Elodie looked at each other. Francesca said, "It was your day yesterday. I get to pick today."

"My" day. We had spent "my" day with me singing to my backpack, which was standing in for the talking clock, while Elodie said "Belle wouldn't say that" and "Those aren't the words to the song."

Francesca looked stormy. I had never challenged her before. If I pushed too hard, I could very well be kicked out of the club. Which meant I would have to hang out by myself in the dirt patch at the end of the playground.

So I said, "What about Sleeping Beauty?" Francesca would be Aurora, but there were a lot of good parts in Sleeping Beauty: the fairies, the mom . . .

Francesca thought about it, then said sweetly, "Okay. But you have to be the witch."

The witch. We never did witches. Supposedly, the whole reason we couldn't do Snow White was because the witch was too scary. In Sleeping Beauty, we always did the scene when the fairies are dancing around getting ready for Aurora's birthday.

Seeing me hesitate, Francesca said, "You're so good at Ursula."

Meaning: You're a good bad guy. You'd be a great witch.

But playing the witch would be like a curse. I knew if I played her this one time, I wouldn't ever get to be a princess again. But if I said no, I still wouldn't get to be a princess, because I'd be kicked out of the club.

So I said, "Okay."

While Francesca and Elodie tried to decide who Elodie would be—Aurora's mom or one of the fairies—I tried to figure out how to do the witch. Her name was Maleficent. Even not knowing what the name meant, I could feel its darkness.

Maleficent gets mad because she's not invited to a party held in Aurora's honor. Listening to Francesca and Elodie chatter away, I understood that I had also been left out. I could still play with them, but only if I played certain roles. Only if I understood that they were the princesses and I was not. I was always going to be the outsider.

3

The accepted but not-quite-as-good. The tolerated, as long as I played by someone else's rules.

However—Maleficent did have black hair. And red lips.

Francesca said, "Let's start when I'm a baby and you come in and curse me."

I felt a fierce desire to do this well. Looking at Francesca curled up on the bench and sucking her thumb, I thought, I'm going to win. I'm going to beat you. You are not going to have the power anymore.

I snatched up a stick, then said to Elodie, "Who dares not let me in?"

Waving her hands in the air, Elodie cried, "Oh, please don't hurt my baby."

"I shall not hurt your baby—yet," I sneered. "But on her sixteenth birthday, she shall prick her finger and fall into a sleep that shall last forever!"

And I pointed the stick at Francesca. "You are doomed." She started crying loud baby sobs.

Then she said, "Okay, let's do the part where I fall asleep."

Francesca loved fainting. Picking up a twig from the ground, she pretended to stab herself in the finger and swooned backward on the bench.

"Sleep," I said in a low voice. "Sleep as if you are dead till the prince comes to waken you."

Francesca giggled, then started to get up.

"No," I said. "Stay down, you're dead."

She looked scornful. "No, I'm not."

"You are. I made you dead." I held the stick out, let it float above her head.

"Sleeping Beauty comes back alive," she argued.

"The prince makes her come back alive." I looked all around the playground to make my point: no prince.

"I'll be the prince," said Elodie quickly.

"No!" I snapped. "No changing. You have to stay what you are."

To Francesca I said, "You can't get up till I say."

And she lay back. I'm not sure why. Either she was genuinely scared of what I might do with that stick or she realized that that's how the story goes. The princess can't rescue herself. As we waited, Francesca uncomfortable on the bench, Elodie standing awkward and bored, I realized that the witch and the prince had the same power over life and death. I could take it away; he could give it back. A princess couldn't do anything.

But the princess gets the prince in the end; the witch goes away and dies. That made me feel strange and lonely at first. Then I noticed Francesca squirming because her legs were too long for the bench. Really, she'd never been my friend. Only now, she had to do what I said.

Ms. Tina called for everyone to come in. Francesca looked at me.

"You're still dead," I told her.

"But my leg hurts," she whimpered.

You made me be the witch, I thought. So this is how it goes.

CHAPTER ONE

HERE'S SOMETHING I DON'T TELL most people.

When I was ten, my dad gave me a small green hippo made of glass with ruby eyes. (That's what I thought at the time. Now I know they're just crystals.) She sat in the palm of my hand, happy and peaceful. I stroked her broad, smooth back with the tip of my finger and said, "This is the nicest thing in the whole world." I named her Mimi, which was what I wished my parents had named me instead of Antonia.

Every year after that, I got another animal. Now there are six and they live on my windowsill. There's Mimi in the center because she was the first. Then Phoebe the unicorn and Dallas the rabbit. Boo Boo is an ape and Gloriana a butterfly. At the very end, Aura the serpent. Aura, I decided long ago, has the most power. I like to keep her a little separate from the others because I'm never quite sure what Aura will do.

The thing I won't tell people—because it's childish, lame, and borderline obsessive-compulsive—is that every day before I leave the house, I sit with my animals and arrange them how they need to be. Each of them has a very different personality—basically, different sides of me—and I like to set them up to give me the best shot at a decent day. For example, if I'm feeling a little lonely and out of it, I'll put shy, awkward Dallas near Gloriana, who's flirty and gorgeous. Mimi is the core me, and a lot of days, I'll put her, Boo Boo, and Phoebe together in a tight group, representing humor, strength, and purity. But if it's going to be one of those "I need you not to mess with me" days, I put Aura in the center. All by herself, because the others are scared of her.

Today is the first day of school. Today Mimi needs her friends around her.

I put her in the center, where the sun can shine on her, put Phoebe and Dallas to her right and left. Boo Boo protects her back; Gloriana is in front to distract her from ugliness.

Aura goes to the corner of the windowsill. I don't want malevolence anywhere near me today.

When I'm done, I put on my backpack and take a deep breath. Then another.

I can't actually breathe all that well.

To distract myself, I look around my room. My messy bed with my purple star quilt. My squashy green chair that used to be in my mom's office. Now Apples, my ancient rag doll, slouches there. On my walls, little promises for the life I want to have someday: a postcard from Venice; a gorgeous black-and-white shot of Dorothy Parker, a sharp-point pen poised at her lips; a shot of people strolling down Fifth Avenue in 1912; Bette Davis, with her sly, knowing look. Someday, I think, I'll be elegant. Fiercely smart. Strong. But still funny, still nice.

I stand in front of the mirror, check out my back-to-school outfit. Cute plaid skirt, plaid bow in the brown hair that seems to be cooperating. Black top, on the tight side. One time, I was at Sephora looking at eye shadow, and the salesman said, "Baby, you got big eyes, big mouth, and big tatas. Work what the good Lord gave you." So I do. At least, I try.

Clothes are fine. What's inside the clothes is a mess. But it'll have to do.

At the last minute, I take out my phone, hoping, praying, whatevering, there is another message. A different message. One that says, Ha, ha, just kidding!

But there isn't. Just the one that came last night. The one that says:

Get ready for hell.

Really—what's the worst that could happen?

This is what I ask myself while I wait for my friend Ella on the corner of Ninety-Fourth and West End.

Get ready for hell.

I try to envision what kind of hell is in store exactly. My mind stretches, tries to feel for the outer reaches of doom. Thick, black, greasy smoke fills my head, seeps down to my stomach until I feel sick.

I won't die, I remind myself. She will not actually kill me.

Probably.

No, okay—realistically, she is not going to kill me. This I know. Or am relatively sure of. I will still be breathing for the next seventy years or so. If I'm not, it won't be because of Chloe Nachmias.

Chloe Nachmias is not going to kill me for real. She doesn't have to.

She can just kill me in all the ways that truly matter when you're starting your junior year of high school.

To distract myself, I look across the street. Two kids standing at the curb. One is maybe my age. He's wearing a black T-shirt. The other's a little younger, like twelve; he's wearing a red hoodie. The light changes, both of them step off the curb.

I think, If red hoodie makes it across first, today will not be a bad day.

Black T-shirt darts ahead, gets to the other side in a flash. I sigh, wishing I didn't believe in signs. But I do, especially when there's a big bucket of caca hanging over my head.

Well, it's a *nice* day, I tell myself. My favorite kind of day. Clear blue sky, a little breeze, the air sharp and fresh. But still warm enough that you can go outside in just jeans and a T-shirt. Usually, I love the first day of school. I love seeing everyone again, hearing the craziness that went on over the summer. The long, hot months away from school turn twerpy boys into broad-shouldered guys. Girls get curves, rad haircuts. People try things over the summer they would never, ever dare in school. So there's a lot to talk about. The five Ws of dirt: who did what where, when, and with whom.

I can't lie. This summer got a little crazy for me. I'd like to say I don't remember some of the things I did. But I do. And so does everyone else. I will definitely be one of the whos discussed.

I would give a lot of money to have that not be true. To have no story anyone's dying to hear. No scoop, no dirt.

No hell.

"Oh, my God, I am *so* sorry!" Ella is stumbling and tumbling toward me, her backpack askew on her shoulders. She is round in all ways—pudgy, curls, moon face—and bounces chaotically through life. She's like a hyper puppy: cute, but you worry someone will kick her.

I haven't seen Ella for two months; she's been at a . . . well, "fat camp" for lack of a nicer term. The New You Health Center. She wasn't allowed to have contact with the outside world, in case someone tried to smuggle Snickers bars through the mail. The camp was her parents' idea; frankly, it sounded kind of cruel. Ella's not that heavy. But food is her drug of choice. And her parents are super-pure stick figures. Eat only fiber. Drink only water. Run a million miles, then do sit-ups till they vomit. Whenever I eat dinner at their house, I get so stressed out with them watching every bite, I want to go directly to Shake Shack afterward. So I get Ella's problem.

Nonetheless, I'm all ready to exclaim, "Oh, my God, you look fantastic! I can't believe how much weight you lost!"

Only Ella looks exactly the same.

She raises her fist ironically. "Six pounds, whoo-hoo!"

"Hey, more than I lost." Which I guess is true if we're only talking weight. Looking for something else to compliment, I notice Ella has a new bag. It has an image of *The Scream,* the Munch painting with the ghostly figure on the bridge holding his face and shrieking.

"Love that," I say.

"Kind of how I feel, right? The camp put me on this insane diet I'm supposed to stay on for my whole entire life." She reaches into the bag, takes out a bag of mini Chips Ahoy. "These aren't exactly on the plan, but hey—first day of school."

She grins. I grin back. Some kids don't like Ella because she never stops talking—usually about somebody else. What they did and who they did it with, why, and man, what do you think will *happen* because oh, my God, this could get really bad. She often communicates with her eyes popped wide open, gasping slightly as if she's out of breath—it's *that* amazing. She lives for what she calls "total drama," as if other people are one big reality show for her to watch and comment on.

But I too like to talk about people. So do most of us, right? The difference between Ella and most of us is Ella doesn't have a mean bone in her body. It would not occur to her to be bitchy; she's so fricking grateful to people for giving her something to talk about, she goes out of her way to be nice about them. Like when Amber Davies showed up for school stoned and it came out that she'd been raiding her parents' pot supply for breakfast, Ella joked, "Man, I'd like some herbal happiness with my low-fat yogurt." Or when Paul Jarrett took up a dare to kiss David Horvath at a party and they kind of sort of ended up making out. Everyone else was all *whisper whisper* because Paul's a major jock with a girlfriend, and now, oh, my God, he's a fag. But Ella just said, "Whoa, good for him. I'd totally swap spit with David, he is H.O.T."

She throws her arms around me. "Oh, my God, so great to see you! Catch me up, I know nothing! What insane naughtiness went on? I must know *everything!*"

Everything, I think. That's a lot.

I nod sideways. *Let's walk*. It's twelve blocks to school. Twelve blocks of safety before the hell.

I decide to start with the most important news. I say lightly, "Well, you know Chloe, right?"

"Super-scary diva bitch Chloe who speaks fluent French and has the wardrobe of life," says Ella promptly. She has everyone at school catalogued in her brain, everything they've ever done and said.

I nod. "And of course Oliver . . ."

"Chloe's super-sweet, brainy boyfriend and you kind of don't get it, but you think, Okay, he's kinky for cruel."

I nod again. "Well, they had this fight over the summer. . . ."

Ella stops dead. She's been friends with me long enough to know where this is going. She mouths "Oh. My. God."

"Yeah," I say unhappily. "A little bit. But it's over, they're back together."

"Is everything cool?"

"Not exactly."

I can say a lot of things in my defense. Yes, Chloe and Oliver have been an official School Super Couple since last winter. But supposedly they were on some kind of sex break, because Chloe'd had this pregnancy scare and wanted to cool it. That was in June. Then in July, Oliver was like, Okay, this has gone on for a while, I'm starting to take it personally, and Chloe was like, Maybe it is personal, I don't know.

He asked, Do you want to break up?

She said, I don't know.

And that's how it was in August when Oliver walked me home from Erica Mittendorf's party. When a guy walks three miles with you on a hot, humid night and you're both making jokes about taking off your clothes and just walking naked and a certain amount of beer has been consumed—

Things happen.

Afterward, we had breakfast at dawn at a diner on Ninety-First Street. I said, "Look, I know you're with Chloe, and my lips are sealed, I promise. I don't want to screw you guys up."

Oliver was quiet for a long time. Then he said, "Actually, I don't know if I *am* with Chloe."

To which I said, "Oh."

"It seems like we're kind of taking a break this summer."

I waited. "But you don't know."

"No."

He looked sad; I felt sad for him. Chloe was Oliver's first girl-friend; everyone knew she had him under her thumb.

Still, I had to ask. "Do you know if the break includes other people?"

He looked at me and we laughed and said at the same time, "No." And I swear, I do not know if we meant no, he didn't know, or no, it didn't include other people.

I said, "This is getting very confused."

"It is," agreed Oliver, and pressed his knee between my legs.

I let it stay confused for about two weeks. But then Lulu Zindel saw us being confused outside a movie theater. That's when it got nasty.

The next day, Oliver called me and said, "Chloe found out. She's pretty upset."

Well, I thought, now we know how Chloe feels about the break-including-other-people question.

"I can imagine," I said. And waited.

Oliver said, "I'm not really sure what to do."

"What do you want to do?" I asked.

And of course he said, "I don't know."

I said, "You should deal with Chloe before anything else happens with us. I think that's fair."

"Probably," said Oliver. "Sorry, this kind of sucks for you."

"Eh," I said lightly, "I'll deal."

And I would have—because I have been through this before. I have deeply weird boyfriend karma. Every guy I've gotten together with has either just broken up with someone or is obsessing about someone else. In eighth grade, Daniel Schrodinger French-kissed me at Carrie Nussbaum's party—not, as it turned out, because he liked me but because he wanted to make Saskia Phelps jealous. I had a total nervous breakdown. *Oh, my God, I thought he liked me and he totally used me—waahhh.*

Same thing in ninth grade when James Olmstead asked me to go out with him the day after Ramona Digby dumped him— and then dumped me two weeks later when Ramona took him back. Tears, tears, tears. Many phone calls to many people. Sob, sob.

But by tenth grade, I knew the score. In tenth grade, when Enzo Carmichal asked me out, I was like, "You and Jane have that whole bestie thing going on. I'm not getting in the middle of that." He was like, "Platonic, dude, platonic."

Now, I knew Jane didn't feel the same way, even though she had never said anything. But I also thought, Well, you know, maybe she needs a push to let him know.

The push worked. About a month after Enzo and I started, Jane got tipsy at a party and tearfully confessed that she was insane about him. Enzo and Jane are still together. She gives me the stink eye whenever I come near them, which is odd, but whatever.

Bottom line: I've learned that freaking gets you nowhere. Stay cool and everybody has more fun.

Yes, I did kind of hope that Oliver was going to break it off with Chloe. And yes, it sucked when it became clear that was not happening. But I dealt with it.

What I couldn't deal with—what I'm still not dealing with so well—is Chloe hating me. And not just Chloe. Her two best friends, Zeena and Isabelle, hate me as well, because, hey, why think for yourself when you can share a brain with two other girls? So much easier! Isabelle and Zeena have been sending me messages too. Highly original and oh-so-witty things like:

Suffer, bitch.

Don't think this is over. It's not.

Oh, and the phone calls. They're fun. Sometimes they're hang-ups. Sometimes not.

Two nights ago, I tried saying, "Chloe, can we talk about this?" Because I didn't want this stuff to still be going on once school started.

Silence.

I said, "I'm really, really sorry. I did not mean for this to happen. I thought you guys had broken up. Now that I know otherwise, I'm out. Okay?"

I thought, She can't be mad now. I said I was sorry. That means I'm saying I was wrong, you were right. Like a dog showing its belly to another dog. *I give up, don't hurt me.*

Then I heard empty silence as she hung up.

So here we are. First day of school and it's still going on. Yay.

"Well, you said Chloe and Oliver made up," says Ella when I'm done with my tale. "So, really, she should be chill."

"Yeah, not so chill," I say unhappily.

I want to tell Ella about the messages Chloe and her psycho posse have been sending. But I realize we're two blocks away from school and I haven't asked Ella anything about *her*. Yes, I am terrified, but that's no excuse for narcissism.

So I say, "How was *your* summer? Was New You total hell or basically bearable?"

Ella goes quiet. Oh, dear, I think, total hell.

Then she says, "Um, this really awful thing happened, actually."

Startled, I stop. "What awful thing?"

"Um—" Ella sighs unhappily. "You know my cousin Cassie?"

Cassie, I think quickly. Ella's cousin who goes to our school, but they never hang out, which is why I don't know her that well. Hard-ass brainiac. Plays rugby and runs with that crowd sometimes. Mostly keeps to herself.

Ella adds, "And my little cousin, Eamonn?"

"No."

Ella shakes her head. "No, duh, why would you? Well, Cassie has this little brother, Eamonn, he's eight and he's like—autistic. Severe. You can't leave him by himself, he's so spastic."

"That's hard," I say.

"Yeah, it is. Or . . . it was. A week ago? He *died*."

My brain goes on the fritz. I can't even think the obvious polite thing to say. All I can think is, Died. Someone died. A little kid *died*. How can I be worried about my stupid crap when a little eight-year-old kid is dead?

Finally I manage to ask, "What happened?"

Ella starts walking again. "I really have no idea. It happened my last week at camp. I didn't find out till I got home and my parents

17

told me. They said he had a seizure or something and drowned in the bathtub. I was like, Why didn't you call me? They were all, Oh, it would have been too upsetting for you—meaning, God forbid you don't lose every last ounce you can. But it sucks. I didn't even get to go to his funeral."

"Were you guys close?"

Ella makes a face. "Um, not amazingly. My mom's super competitive with Cassie's mom, and there's always drama, drama. And Eamonn was cute but a little hard to be around. Still . . ."

Still, you want to be included in your own family. I nod. "Your poor cousin," I say. "Was she there when it happened?"

"Yeah, she was," says Ella. "In fact, she was supposed to be taking care of him. Their parents weren't home."

"Oh, God. She must feel awful."

"I wouldn't know," says Ella. "Everyone's like, Don't bring it up, whatever you do! My mom said, Your aunt and uncle are very fragile right now, leave them be. Cassie won't share with me, she thinks I'm a grade-A moron. Which, you know, maybe I am, but she could be nicer about it. All I heard was that she wants everyone to call her Cassandra now. No more Cassie."

Weirdly, I get that. Wanting to be a different person after something awful happens to you. Thinking, Yeah, everything'll be fine if I'm not the person who went through that hideous crap.

Maybe I should change my name too. We're a block away from school now. It'd be nice to be able to say, "The craziness this summer? The Oliver/Chloe drama? No, that was some other girl. Toni, yeah. I'm not her. I'm . . . Anastasia."

At the last crossing, I think, If the light changes to green before I count to five, I will be safe. If it changes after five, I am in danger.

One, two, three . . .
Please change, I think. Seriously, universe. Do me a favor.
Four, five . . . six . . . seven . . .
It goes green.
I am so screwed.

CHAPTER TWO

OUR SCHOOL IS THE DEKALB Community School. It was started by professors at DeKalb University so they'd have a cheap private school to send their kids to, although they've started letting nonstaff kids in if they pay more. My dad teaches history at DeKalb, which is why I'm here. Ella's mom teaches math, her dad economics—which Ella says makes her feel even stupider than she is.

Our building used to be an old Catholic school. My mom says that when they moved in, the place was "a horror," with green walls and dark stairways with metal stairs, that felt like a prison. There were all these crosses and religious statues in the classrooms. "All these saints in death agony and Marys on the half shell," my mom says.

DeKalb got rid of the statues, painted all the walls white, and replaced the Join the Jesuits posters with Clean Up Your Community! signs. They threw out the old wood desks and replaced them with big, round white tables. The windows are big, the rooms bright and sunny. There are Smart Boards in all the class-rooms. The cafeteria serves organic food. You look at the kids in the halls, chattering away, and you can't believe this was ever a place with nuns, crosses, and black robes, where everyone was obsessed with sinning and death and God's ultimate judgment.

Outside the entrance, there's a plaza encircled by plants and shrubs. Right now, it's packed with kids. As I walk through the crowd and into school on this first day of my junior year, I wonder, Is Chloe already inside? Are her friends with her? Are they waiting for me?

Get ready for hell.

I only have to survive for half a day, I tell myself as we wade into the crowded lobby. The first day of school starts at eight-thirty and ends at twelve. You have to be in your homeroom by nine. The Welcome Back to School assembly for juniors starts at ten. Then you register for classes, and you're done. Nearly everything that happens today takes place in a crowd. Chloe is not in my homeroom; neither are her friends. So the only times I will be truly vulnerable are bathroom breaks. Hopefully, I can make it to lunchtime without taking one.

As Ella and I head up the stairs to the juniors' lockers, Ella mutters, "I know what everyone's going to think: She spent two months at a fat camp, and she's still a blimp?"

"Stop," I tell her. "You look great."

But it's true. Most of us have known one another since diapers, so the first day of school provides the only real surprises. As I hug people hello, compliment new clothes or summer tans, tease, and ask questions, I register changes. Huh, Karen got the long-discussed nose job. Oh, David Fink got his braces off, confidence has soared. Leslie Davis looks fantastic. Jason Arnstein looks more depressed than ever. He really needs a new shrink.

And I know they're looking at me and wondering if what they heard about me over the summer is true. I can feel the questions swirling like spirits. So I just keep the focus on whoever I'm talking to: "God, love the hair." "Where'd you go in August?" "The summer reading was insane!" I don't give anyone room to ask questions—especially about Oliver. With Chloe on the rampage, the worst thing I could do is talk about him. It would sound like bragging or whining or some hellacious combination of both. What happens in summer stays in summer.

But as I'm trying to figure out my locker combination, Nina Watts catches me off guard, saying, "Yo, heard someone had a hot summer."

I glance up at her, wondering what she's heard. Her face shows intense interest but no clues. I shrug casually. "Really kinda lukewarm."

"No deets?" She puts out her lower lip.

"No fun ones. Sorry."

She walks away disappointed. I wonder if it might have been a good idea to give her just a few deets. Then I could have asked her some questions. Like, What are people saying about me? Think I'm a total slut?

And—pathetically—Does everyone still like me?

It seems like they do. Later, Xander Bartlett waggles his eyebrows and asks, "Did you seriously flash a bunch of cars on the Fifty-Ninth Street Bridge?" I give him an "And you missed it" smile.

A few minutes after, Malaya Chen squeals, "Oh, my God, I heard you proposed to an NYU guy at Ping Pong Rocks." I joke, "Rumors, rumors—and he was Columbia."

So far, everyone is . . . friendly. No one has said, You bitch, you tried to steal Chloe's boyfriend.

Of course, I haven't run into Chloe yet.

Not all the gossip is about me. On my way to homeroom, I hear Tessa Sedgewick say to Becca Lewes, "God, did you hear her brother died?" and I know they're talking about Cassie.

And Becca says, "I saw her in the hallway. No big tears. She's totally bizarro."

Maybe it's my stress about my sitch, but this really pisses me off. I want to say, "Yeah, how *should* you act when your little brother dies?" I've never gotten why we double Xs are so bitchy about each other. It's like, We're half the population, people. Chill.

In homeroom, I get some sideways looks and *whisper-whispers* from certain people. Whatever, I think. At least no one's mentioned Oliver. As long as that stays quiet, Chloe won't feel humiliated. Then maybe she'll let it go.

My homeroom teacher is Mr. Emmersdorf. He teaches French, and he's kind of lingo-Asperger's in that things that take place in English don't really register. As he drones on about the key events of September, Wallace Laird leans over to me and whispers, "Brave female."

I give him a puzzled look. Generally, I'm a proud member of the Chicken Poop Club.

Wallace peers at me over his glasses. "Messing with Chloe Nachmias? Crazy brave. You bring your brass knuckles to school?"

I pat my bag like, Yep, got 'em right here. But my stomach starts churning. If Wallace is talking about me and Oliver, then everyone is. If Wallace expects Chloe to kick my ass, that improves the chances of Chloe kicking my ass by about one hundred percent. Considering the chances were fairly high before, this is not good.

People do not cross Chloe. The girl just holds on to anger. Like, we all get pissed and say "God, I hate that person," or "I'm totally done with so-and-so." And maybe "You bitch" behind their back, but nothing more. Chloe takes hate to a whole other level. Chloe's very popular; when she's not on the warpath, she can be a funny, cool person. She's a school star. Even if you don't like her, you secretly hope that one day she'll like you.

But I notice her two best friends, Isabelle and Zeena, are total doormats who go along with whatever she says. That's because the reasons Chloe decides to hate people can be . . . mysterious, let's say that.

For example. Chloe used to be best friends with Hannah Nigh. They did student council; one of them came up with the idea to have a fund-raising dance for . . . sorry, some country that had a big earthquake, I don't remember which one. And Chloe said it was her idea and Hannah said it was hers, and the knives came *out*. For a while, it was total war between them. Then Hannah got over it. Chloe didn't.

If Hannah came into a room, Chloe would immediately leave or move to the farthest point from her. She never said her name again, always referred to her as the Bitch Who Shall Not Be Named. If Hannah was invited to something, you could not invite Chloe, unless you wanted things thrown. A year later, Chloe still gets all angry cat and hisses, "Well, you know what she did to me," whenever Hannah's name comes up.

This isn't the first time Chloe's decided she hates my guts. In eighth grade, we did a history project together. Since my dad's a history professor and I sometimes "help" him with research, Chloe figured we'd ace it. I'm just not an ace-it kind of person. And frankly, she was so intense about it, she wigged me out. So I put it off and ended up doing my half at the last minute.

We got a B. Chloe never spoke to me after that. She'd walk by me in this sniffy, offended way like, You know what you did, and I was like, Uh, no, I don't, actually.

So this is the girl I've pissed off. Did I mention I'm not terribly bright sometimes?

"Bon!" announces Mr. Emmersdorf. *"Venez, s'il vous plaît, à la réunion."* Mr. Emmersdorf, I want to say, I am barely passing Spanish. Do not throw French at me as well.

Not today.

Just before I enter the stairwell to head to the gym, I realize that there is no way I will make it through an hour of school spirit if I don't take a serious piss. The girls' bathroom is right nearby. I'm not going in alone. I see Abby Cronin go in. For a moment, I hesitate. Abby is best buds with Dahlia Carraway, whose ex, Dylan, hooked up with me after they broke up. Dahlia apparently thought she had dibs on Dylan for the rest of their lives, and she was upset. Whatever.

I'm sure Abby's not my biggest fan. But she's not tight with Chloe and her fashionistas—and they can hardly attack me if she's there. So this is safer than a bathroom where I don't know who's inside. I follow her in.

Unlike the rest of the school, the bathrooms are still old-fashioned. The sinks are low, the enamel cracked. The mirrors are spotted and dull. The stalls are a hideous shade of puke-green. It's like a portal to the old Catholic school. I feel like I should be wearing a black skirt and white blouse.

At the sinks, I try "Hey, Abby."

"Hi," she says—cool, but not actively hostile.

"Good summer?"

She gives a "We're not really friends so I'm not going to tell you" shrug. I smile back like, Yeah, don't actually care, it's called manners.

Then she says, "*You* had a good summer, by all accounts." "By all accounts": This is the kind of phrase Abby uses to make you feel she's wise. You want to say, Actually, Abby, it's just pretentious as F.

Dabbing on lip gloss, I say, "Erm, lot of ups, lot of downs."

She turns, suddenly bristling. "Oh, yeah? Which was Oliver?"

Startled by her anger, I stammer, "Um—over?"

"Is it really?" she demands.

"Yes," I tell her, resisting the urge to say, And this is your business . . . why?

For a moment, we focus on our reflections. Then Abby mutters, "I mean, I'm sorry, but I just don't think you realize the pain you cause people."

I am totally thrown. Abby's acting like I make a habit of dating taken guys, which I absolutely do not. I try to come up with some nasty, devastating retort, but all I can think of is she thinks I do this on purpose. Like I want to hurt people. She has some mean, evil slut in her mind—and thinks that's me. And it's not, it's so not. . . .

And that's really all I want to tell her. But Abby flounces out of the bathroom before I can.

I pat a cold paper towel on my face and try to calm down. I

tell myself that Abby is crazy. Jealous. Thwarted. A total B and a half. If she hates me, so be it. If she thinks whatever about me, it doesn't mean the rest of the school thinks the same. Her feelings cannot hurt me.

Still, I feel those emotions, red and hateful, like heat on my back, as I hurry toward the stairs.

I make it to the gym just before assembly. I am weak with relief to see Ella, and I fling myself into the seat next to hers. "Hey." She smiles and rubs my arms.

The auditorium is filling up. Kids wander the aisles, looking for seats. Ella munches the last of her Chips Ahoys and glances around. "You haven't seen Chloe, have you?"

I shake my head.

"Good. Because I heard—"

She hesitates.

"What?"

But whatever it is Ella heard, I don't get to hear it, because Mr. Crosbie, the headmaster, taps the microphone; it makes a huge, ugly electronic screech—I would too if Mr. Crosbie touched me—and everyone cracks up. The Welcome Back to School assembly for juniors has begun.

The back-to-school assembly for juniors is essentially, Whatever you do, remember *college*! College, college, college. Oh, and did we mention college? By the way, don't forget college. One last thing—*College!* I want to scream, College? Let me get through this day, okay?

When Mr. Crosbie's done with the Remember to Put Every Fart on Your Resume speech, he says, "I would like us all to rise and join hands, please. We will now recite the school civility pledge."

Normally, the pledge is major oog as far as I'm concerned. But right now, I'll take any nudges toward niceness I can get. I take Ella's hand and offer my other to Bill "Pigman" Pullman on my right. He grins maniacally, like I've offered him some other body part to touch. I say, "Drooling's not pretty, Bill."

Mr. Crosbie's voice rings out over the gym, followed by a grimy murmur as we repeat his words. "I pledge to be civil and caring to my fellow students. To create a welcoming environment free of hostility and prejudice."

I pray that Chloe is listening.

After assembly, we trudge back downstairs to the cafeteria to register for classes. There are a million people on the stairs, and the crowd moves sluggishly. Chloe couldn't reach me—but I could be crushed to death in a stampede.

The cafeteria isn't big enough to hold the whole class, so you have to wait on line in the hallway until it's your turn to go in. It's only the first day of school, but I swear it smells of old chicken soup. There are no teachers in the outside hallway; they're all inside registering kids. Every so often, the door opens and Ms. Davenport, the dean, calls out, "Next ten!" But that's it for supervision.

I keep a close eye on the door, nervous that at any minute Chloe will come out, her two flunkies in tow.

Then Lizbeth Dawson comes up to me and Ella. Lizbeth is the captain of the rugby team. She has a face full of freckles and a wide smile. Lizbeth is real people. Everyone likes her and she likes everybody. I relax, knowing she's not here to read me the slut act.

She says to Ella, "Did I hear about some sadness in your family?"

Gulping in surprise that someone as popular as Lizbeth would speak to her, Ella says, "Yeah, my little cousin. He died."

Lizbeth frowns in sympathy. "Can you tell Cass I'm really sorry? And if she wants, call me?"

"Sure," says Ella. "But you can—"

Lizbeth shakes her head. "I tried. She doesn't seem to want to talk right now. But I wanted her to hear I care, you know?"

"Sure, yeah," says Ella nodding. Then when Lizbeth leaves, she mutters, "You're just getting the Cassie treatment, sorry to say."

"The Cassie treatment?" I ask.

"Oh—" But before she can explain, Ms. Davenport calls "Next ten!" and it's our turn. Inside, it's a total mob scene, people shoving and elbowing to get to the lines for popular classes. Ella says to me, "I don't see Chloe. Big phew, huh?"

"Chill," I say, because her nerves are making me nervous. If I'm going to run into Chloe anywhere, it'd be here.

We register for English first. I think, If I can get Ms. Davis's class on African American literature and avoid Mr. Rhinehart's class on Elizabethan poetry, the universe is on my side and I will be okay.

"Sorry, sweetie," says Ms. Padalla when I get to the table. "African American's all filled up. How about some Spenser?"

Once we're done with English, Ella goes to sign up for French while I sign up for Spanish and twentieth-century history. While I'm stuck on line, Ella finds me and says, "I have to talk to the administration about my gym exemption." Ella gets a note from her doctor claiming she has a knee problem and can't take gym. Every year, the school hassles her about it, which they should because it is kind of crap. Or maybe I'm just jealous my doctor won't make up a knee problem for me so I can get out of gym too.

Then she asks, "Meet by the lockers after this and go for ice cream?"

"Are you allowed on this crazy diet?"

"First day of school," she explains patiently.

I say "Sure" and hope she doesn't hear how scared I am to be on my own.

Once I've registered for history, I'm done. Alone, I feel the space around me expand and empty out. I glance around for Nina, Malaya, anybody—but there's not one person I can attach myself to.

Then I spot Oliver, waiting on line for World Humanity. That's a special class in . . . making the world better, I think. You do ecology and economics and general save-humanity stuff. Oliver's into all that. His dad teaches Chinese and his mom works for the UN. Oliver is super-serious brainy man—whereas I'm a "got no clue, just trying to get through" kind of girl. Over the summer, he told me that the World Humanity class is a good way to get a summer job with Amnesty International. In fact, he has his first interview for the Amnesty gig in a month. He's horrendously nervous about it.

He really is adorable.

Do not talk to him, I tell myself. Do not. It will be all over school in five seconds and Chloe will have even more reason to hate you.

But if I just walk past him, that's not talking to him, is it? If he talks to me, that's his choice, right?

I have to do this smart. Keep my eye focused on something else, as if I haven't even noticed he's there.

Toni, hey—

It only happens in my head. I walk near him. . . .

Walk past him.

He says nothing. Absolutely nothing.

I know he saw me. I can tell by the way he stared straight ahead as I passed.

Crap, Oliver. Seriously?

Behind me, I hear a giggle. The kind of murmur that tells you people are talking about you. Then laughter . . .

I am not, not, not going to let anyone see me cry.

I race into the nearest bathroom, praying no one is in there. I'm in luck. Most kids are either still registering or they have stronger bladders than I do. I sit in the stall, try not to feel like the saddest, biggest loser on the planet.

I feel so effing stupid. It is a basic rule. Guys who are half of a super couple always, always, go back to their girlfriends. I know this. I should not have expected Oliver to do anything other than what he did.

Although I did expect him to act like a human being.

Whatever. All I can do is move on.

I go to the sink, smack my face with a wet paper towel, and blink a million times. Then I brush my hair as hard as I can. Then I retie my hair bow and go back into the world.

Just in time to see Chloe, Isabelle, and Zeena coming down the hall.

I take a deep breath. Think, So, here we are.

One summer, when I was having trouble with creeps on the street commenting on my anatomy, my mom gave me a piece of advice. "Show no fear," she said. "Act like they're not there. Do not let them see that you're nervous or upset. If you look like a victim, you have a much greater chance of becoming a victim." After that, I put on my most badass face when I walked down the street. And it actually worked. The "Oh baby, babys" stopped.

Now I tell myself, Act like they're not there. Show no fear whatsoever.

Chloe is petite and perfect. She stands around five foot nothing, and every part is ideal, from her toned arms to the legs that look great in short skirts. She never looks an ounce over- or underweight. She wears her dark hair in a French braid most of the time. She always makes me feel clumsy and unwashed. Isabelle is dark with a bony, model body and Zeena is a short, plump blonde who likes to work a rich-girl sneer.

There are two doors in every hallway, one to the west stairway, the other to the east. Chloe and her friends are blocking the east stairway. I give them a quick smile, start heading to the west stairs. But Isabelle and Zeena get there first. Now I'm stuck in the middle of the hall, with the three of them—well, basically surrounding me.

Chloe says sweetly, "Isabelle, remind me, aren't we supposed to give Toni something?"

"Did it start with an . . . 'H'?" Isabelle wonders.

"End with an 'L'?" adds Zeena.

"*That's* what we meant to give her," croons Chloe. "Hell."

As one, they start walking toward me. I am cornered, trapped between the wall and them. I look to each door, praying someone will bust in and save me. But everyone's at registration or long gone. I think of Mimi at home on the windowsill. How I surrounded her with friends, put her enemy far away. That was supposed to protect me. So why am I surrounded by enemies?

Chloe stops in front of me. Isabelle steps left, Zeena right. A single word out of my mouth will be the signal to attack. I feel their eyes, their excitement. Chloe's hate.

They close in on me.

They start to whisper, one after the other. Chloe, then Zeena, then Isabelle. "*Everyone knows. Everyone knows. Everyone knows.*" Their voices blend, grow louder as they speak as one.

"*Everyone knows. Everyone knows. Everyone knows.*"

I draw in a ragged gulp of air and break through. Without looking back, I walk quickly toward the nearest exit. Pretend I don't hear Chloe say in that creepy singsong voice, "Don't go. We have so much more to give you. . . ."

They didn't hurt me, I think as I pound up the stairs. I was never actually in danger. They just wanted me to feel like I was.

Maybe that'll be it, I tell myself. Maybe they just wanted to scare me a little and they'll be satisfied with that. I mean, really. What else are they going to do?

The school has pretty much emptied out. Ella and I are supposed to meet by our lockers. All I have to do is make it up to the fourth floor. But when I get to the doorway, I hear the rattle of a locker and freeze. They followed me, Chloe and her poseur posse. They're waiting just beyond this door in that empty hallway. Because now everyone's gone home and they can do whatever they want. . . .

Cautiously, I look through the wire grill window in the door.

And see Cassie.

No, Cassandra now.

I should just leave her alone. If this day has been weird for me, I can only imagine what it's been like for her.

Even before now, Cassandra's always kept her distance from most kids at school. Her dad is a poet, her mom is a philosophy professor. Cassandra is smart—and she comes off as a little . . . pure, somehow. I always imagine she goes somewhere after school and talks about Kierkegaard or something. She's also quite tall. As the Sephora guy might say, the good Lord didn't do too bad by her. She's got wide shoulders and big, springy brown hair she wears short around her face. She has a long, strong jawline, a full mouth, and huge, catlike eyes. My dad's specialty is FDR, and Cassandra looks like Eleanor Roosevelt's pretty cousin, if you can imagine that.

I peek through the window again. I wonder if anyone was nice to her today.

Someone really should be nice to her.

Carefully, I step through the door.

Immediately, Cassandra turns. Those amazing green-gray eyes. They hit me like a spotlight. I feel caught, immediately guilty. I fight the urge to squint. Or even run.

Which may be why I stammer. "I-I'm sorry."

She's still staring at me. Waiting.

"I heard about what happened," I say.

She frowns slightly, shakes her head.

I swing my book bag uselessly. "Ella told me about your brother."

This was probably a mistake, mentioning Ella. Getting more uncomfortable by the second, I add, "Anyway, I'm really sorry."

Cassie/Cassandra doesn't say anything.

"So, ciao," I say, and start walking back to the stairwell. I can wait for Ella outside.

But as I do, I sense Cassandra behind me, sense her watching. Her gaze is hot, prickly between my shoulders. I fight the urge to scratch.

Stop, I think. Chill out.

But I can't. The spot between my shoulders is burning now; the laser's cut through the cloth, is searing my skin. Panicky, I reach back.

Feel nothing. Soft, dull cotton.

I hear Cassandra laugh, high and joyful—Made you look!—and spin around.

Screw you! I scream in my head. I was trying to be nice.

But she's not there. The hallway's empty.

The chick is weird, I tell myself as I wait on the street for Ella. Everyone's always said that about Cassandra. Even when she did the same things everyone else did, liked the same stuff, you always felt she was faking it a little.

I guess she's stopped faking.

And frankly, screw her for making me feel this stupid.

I look at the time. And screw Ella for being late. Again.

And Oliver.

Oh, and obviously Chloe.

And Isabelle. And Zeena.

And Abby.

And Nina and Wallace and everyone who's obsessed with my supposed slutdom.

In fact, let's just say screw everybody.

Screw. Them. All.

CHAPTER THREE

"**WHAT'D YOU DO IN SCHOOL** today?"

If you ever hang out at my house for a while, you will hear this question. A lot. It is a very important question to my parents. And please note: It is not How was school today? which is what most parents ask. Or even What happened in school today? It's What did *you*—Antonia Thurman—do in school today? What smart thing did you say? What good deed did you perform? What friend did you make? What teacher did you impress?

Which may be why I usually say, Nothing.

We are eating dinner. We don't really have a dining room, just what my mom calls an "eating nook," a round white table with four chairs just off the kitchen. Over our heads is a large orange glass lamp that shines only on the table. We haven't turned on the living room lights; most of the house is dark. So it feels like we're castaways, huddled around the fire on a desert island.

My mom says, "Must have been nice to see your friends."

I nod, thinking, Um, yes, except that they've decided I'm a man-stealing whore.

Then my dad asks my mom, "How'd that billing thing with your patient go?"

My mom waves her hand. "Problem solved. Everything's fine."

Everything's fine. That's another thing you hear around my house a lot. My mom says it on the phone when she's talking to friends. My dad says it to his brother when he's asked how it's going. They both say it to me. Not the actual words, so much. But in their frozen smiles, the happy talk at the dinner table, the way my dad sits hunched and quiet while my mom chatters on—it's all *Everything's fine!*

I look at the fourth chair. I don't know why we have four, when there are only three of us. For guests, I guess. Except we haven't had anyone over lately.

I look over at my dad. I wonder if he's thinking about Katherine.

Another way you know "everything's fine"? You never, ever hear the name Katherine in our house.

Last year, you heard it a lot. Katherine the savior. Katherine the miracle worker. Katherine, my dad's graduate assistant, who was such a huge help to my dad and even my mom, because she did things around the house. Not only did she answer the phone so my dad could work, help him with research, and do clerical junk, she picked up dry cleaning, shopped, and kept track of my mom's schedule too. My mom once said Katherine was like some good fairy who had decided to live in our house and work magic with a wave of her wand.

This was, of course, before we knew that Katherine and my dad were having a . . . whatever.

No, that's not fair. I can't call it a whatever, it was more than that. It went on for almost a year. And I'm not entirely sure? But I think my dad was in love with Katherine. Katherine was definitely in love with him. That I know—because she told me.

It was a Sunday afternoon in June. My mom got this weird impulse to drive to Westchester to see old friends. Like, all of a sudden: We must see David and Pauline! I wanted to stay home. So I said, That's nice, you kids have a good time.

My dad wanted to stay home too. He pointed out to my mom that it was Sunday and Sunday was his day to play basketball at the Y. But she said, "Skip it."

Usually when my mom says skip it, my dad skips.

But this time he said, "I don't like to let people down, Claire."

"Okay. Then don't let me down," said my mom, her voice tight and angry. "Skip it."

There was this long, ugly silence. Then my dad shrugged. "Okay."

Even at the time, I wondered why they were getting so weird about one afternoon. But then I remembered the general rule that all parents are insane and forgot about it.

As I said, my dad's a historian, and every so often he drags me into one of his research projects, I'm guessing to build up my academic bona fides. That week, I was supposed to be looking up some facts about the WPA. Only I decided I deserved the day off.

So I was sitting on the couch, catching up on *True Blood*, when the door buzzer rang. Walking to the door, I thought, Maybe it's a deranged psycho killer come to murder me.

Peeking through the hole, I saw Katherine.

My parents are dead, I thought instantly. They had an accident. Katherine's here to tell me they're dead.

Opening the door, I said, "Hey, what's up?"

For the record, I liked Katherine. She was like a cool big sister. Usually my dad's assistants threw me a hey or hello, then ignored me totally. Katherine treated me like a bud, joking with me, asking me where I shopped. It felt good to get compliments from her, because Katherine had it together. She had long brown hair and big gray eyes, and you could tell she ran and swam because she enjoyed it, not just to get a banging bod—although she did happen to have a banging bod. I always wondered if it was the exercise that made her so up and positive. Like if I ran ten miles a day, I'd feel that strong and confident too.

But Katherine wasn't looking so together. Her eyes were red, her arms folded tightly. She was wearing a nice skirt, but it was wrinkled, and the T-shirt looked like she had pulled it out of the wash bin. Her hair was pulled back with two combs, but it was coming loose. Strands of hair hung limp around her face. Her lips were chapped, as if she'd been chewing on them.

This is bad, I thought. Really bad.

Then she said, "Hi, Tone." She was straining to keep her voice normal. "Is, uh, your dad here?"

I felt immediate relief. If she was asking about my dad, she was not here to tell me he was dead.

"No. He and my mom went to Westchester."

"Westchester?" She said it like she had never heard of the place.

"To see friends." I opened the door wider. "Do you want to come in, by the way?"

She wandered in, still lost in her thoughts. For a few moments, she stared around the apartment, as if making sure my dad wasn't hiding someplace. She noticed a row of family photos on the side table in the dining room. She picked up a recent shot of my mom and dad, laughing with their arms around each other. Then she set it down, hard.

"What's in Westchester?" she asked bluntly.

"Friends. My mom wanted to go." I don't know why I felt like I had to add that. But I was nervous. I didn't know this harsh, unfriendly Katherine.

She frowned. Then muttered, "Well, that's just great. He—"

I said, "What?"

Turning, she said in a loud voice, "I was about to say, he was supposed to see me."

Puzzled, I said, "He does basketball Sundays. . . ."

She laughed. A short, ugly bark. *"Basketball—"*

Now she was making fun of me. It was clear: Katherine was here to fight.

She laughed again. "Basketball. Jesus Christ."

Annoyed, I said, "Yeah, basketball. Big round orange ball goes into the net."

"Yeah," she said dismissively. "Henry doesn't play basketball."

Henry? What happened to Professor Thurman? "Sorry, he does. Only not today because, like I said—"

"He's in Westchester," she finished for me.

"Right."

"But all those other Sundays he was playing basketball," she said, pleasant-nasty.

One thing I hate? When people want to tell you something, but they don't just come out and say it, because it's not a *nice* thing and they're supposedly *nice* people. So they go *blah blah blah* and expect to get points for being sweet when really they're kicking your ass.

Wanting to push her into a place where the claws would come out, I said, "Look, Katherine, is there something you're saying here?"

"What do you *think* I'm saying?" she asked sarcastically.

"Honestly, I have no idea."

She gave me an exasperated look, like I was the dumbest creature on the planet. "Basketball. I cannot believe that's what he told you. I mean, of all the lame, stupid lies . . ."

Then she did a weird double take. As if she'd been sleepwalking and just woken to realize someone—me—was in the room. Her mouth twisted up and her eyes started leaking tears. "Oh, God," she said in a strangled voice. "Oh, God, I'm sorry."

Utterly confused, I said, "No, it's okay."

She sank into one of the dining room chairs. "You must hate me. Saying these crazy things. I don't know what I was thinking."

All of a sudden, I understood. Not the words, but what they meant. That everything was completely different than I thought it was. That Katherine was a different person. My dad was a different person. That they had this whole life, this whole other reality, and I didn't have the first clue.

In a tiny voice, Katherine whispered, "Just, I love him, and I don't know what to do."

That's when the images started. What the word "love" really

means: Basically, two people naked and getting sweaty as they hump all over each other. And one of them was my fifty-four-year-old dad.

I thought of him. Weak. Desperate. Grateful. My stomach turned over.

I bet he's really into her, I thought numbly. Look at her. There is no way he chooses us over that.

Everything in me twisted like piano wire, tight and deadly. I started vomiting words like "Get out, I fucking hate you, get out." When I ran out of words, I just screamed, as if I could blast her out of the apartment. Katherine scrambled up from the couch, pathetic and scared as she blubbered, Yes, yes, absolutely. Her fear made me feel powerful, and I practically chased her to the door, hurling every ugly name I could think of as she flung I'm sorrys back at me like used Kleenex.

Then she was gone. I fell into one of the dining room chairs and thought, Okay. What now?

It doesn't seem possible that I could have done nothing but wander from room to room all afternoon, buzzing and blank like a broken TV. Maybe I knew that if I did anything more complicated—opened the refrigerator, took a walk in the park—my brain would have to switch itself back on.

At one point, I decided to take a bath. Sliding into the full tub, I looked down at my belly, white and trembling under the water. My thighs enormous, my chest bobbing half above the surface. Every part of me felt swollen and sensitive and disgusting. I clawed at my stomach and inside thighs, trying to rip the soft fat away. Bone. I wanted pure, hard, unfeeling bone.

But in the end, I couldn't do it. I bunched up my wet hair in front of my face and cried. I let myself slide under the water; my hair floated up and away. If you rise up, it will choke you, I told myself. Stay down. Stay down.

Of course I didn't. I've never been good at holding my breath.

Katherine, in the meantime, was calling my dad. I'm sure she thought she was doing the right thing; that's usually what people who screw up your life tell themselves. Later, my mom told me she knew something was wrong when my dad said he had to take a call right in the middle of lunch—and he went outside to take it. She worried it was me. That something had happened. Which it had, but it had happened to her too.

After a while, my dad came back to the table and said with a big smile, "Everything's fine. False alarm."

But on the drive home, he told my mom the truth.

I don't know what happened in that car. When my mom came home, she was alone. I was hiding under the covers.

My mom came straight back to my room and gathered me up.

"Everything's going to be okay," she murmured to me. "Everything is going to be just fine. . . ."

"Henry?"

It's the second time my mom's said it. Only now my dad hears her and looks up. "Hand me the pepper?" she asks.

"Certainly." He reaches, gives it to her.

Though we never talk about her, Katherine is still with us. You can feel her in the air, hear her in the silences. But if we keep talking to each other, fill up the house with sound, there will be no room for her.

"Thank you, darlin'."

"You're welcome, sweetie."

It's supposed to be a joke, my parents using these fake country accents. So I add, "Aw, shucks, honey."

My mom smiles. "So, seriously. First day back. Scale of one to ten?"

My dad nods, as if he suddenly remembered. "School. Yes. Tell us."

This time, I will not be able to say "Nothing." My mom is asking me to keep things going, to make sure the little drifts of Katherine won't pull together, take shape, and gain power.

So I think of what happened today at school.

Get ready for hell.

The girls closing in on me. *Everyone knows.*

I should tell them about that.

Only there's no way I can. Because here's what would happen: My mom would demand, Why would these girls do this to you? What is wrong with them? My dad would march to the phone to call Chloe's family. My mom would rant about bullying, kids who pick on kids for no reason.

And in the end, I'd have to say, Well, uh, not exactly no reason. I kind of messed around with her boyfriend.

After that, I imagine silence. As we all think about that other person, the one who messed with our lives this summer. All that anger and hatred Mom and I have for her. How would my mom feel if she thought I did the same thing as Katherine?

My mom would want to still call the school, still yell at Chloe's parents. But all along, I bet she'd be feeling it was my fault. While my dad would think it was his fault. And I'd know, really, the whole damn sorry mess was my fault.

"Fine," I tell my mom. "It was fine. A definite seven at least."

That night, I'm lying in bed trying to figure out how I'm going to get through the rest of my life when my phone buzzes.

Text message from Ella. *I suck! Sorry! Meeting took forever! Yogurt on me?*

Yep, I think, tossing the phone down. You do suck, Ella. Not always. But sometimes.

Almost as soon as it hits the blanket, the phone buzzes again. I am just so popular.

This message is from Chloe. It also starts with *Sorry!*

My heart leaps. It's over. They got what they wanted, realized they were wrong. Because they're not heinous people, they're basically okay. . . .

I read.

Sorry! We made you a promise. We promised you hell—but we really didn't give it to you today. Our bad. We'll make it up to you tomorrow, we promise.

Sleep tight!

I will kill her, I think. Seriously. I have had it with this crap. Tomorrow, I will . . .

Will . . .

The three of them pressing in on me. So thrilled that they could scare me.

I have to not be scared, I tell myself.

My phone buzzes again. Furious, I snatch it up. If it's Chloe, I am texting her back this time.

But it's Cassandra. She must have gotten my number from the school directory.

She writes

Sorry. I know you were trying to be nice.

Of course it doesn't take a psychic to know that's what I was trying to do. It's not like Cassandra read my mind or anything.

So why does it feel like she did?

CHAPTER FOUR

THE NEXT DAY ON THE way to school, I make a decision. Summer did not happen. Katherine, the parties, Oliver—none of it. And if other people want to see it differently, that's their problem.

At first, it seems to work. I hit the lockers, go to homeroom, then head to my first class. Nobody crowds me. No one insults me. We're all just doing our thing.

Good, I think. Maybe it was just the first day. Now everybody's over it.

In the afternoon, I spot Chloe on my way to science. I stiffen, will myself to keep walking. Chloe sees me, too. For a split second, our eyes meet. Then she turns to the girl she's with—Elana something—and whispers.

Elana something stares at me.

I take a deep breath, keep moving. So, Chloe's trashing me to kids I don't know and don't care about. I can live with that.

But the next day, in art class, a group of girls suddenly goes silent when I pass them on my way to the pottery wheel. Behind me, I hear *bzz, bzz.*

It could be not about me.

But it probably is. I tell myself I don't care.

That afternoon, Nina coos, *"Sure* you don't want to dish about the summer?"

"I was in Maine all summer," I tell her. "I got bitten by a tick, went into a coma, and woke up the day school started."

Nina grins. "Well, you better check in with your coma self. She got pretty wild while you were out."

The next day, I find a condom taped to my locker, with a note: "Thought you could use this."

Cute, I think. Very cute.

In the cafeteria, giggles from a table of girls as I pass. Charming grunting noises from a table of guys. I decide to eat lunch out for a while.

The next day at lunchtime, I tell Ella I have a mad craving for pizza and want to go out. She says quickly, "Yeah, that's a good idea."

She's quiet on the walk over to Ray's. It occurs to me that Ella is the one person who isn't asking me about the summer. Ella, who lives for gossip.

The gossip must be pretty bad.

I get two slices. Thinking of the diet she's supposed to be on, Ella hesitates, then says, "I'll join you," and gets two as well. I wonder if she wants to keep her mouth full so she won't have to tell me the truth.

As we squeeze into a tiny booth, I say, "Okay. Tell me."

Ella frowns, takes a bite of pizza. "What?"

"What are people saying?" She hesitates. "Ella, I can handle it."

"I know."

"So, tell me."

And she does. She doesn't want to, so the stories come slowly. The flashing on the Fifty-Ninth Street Bridge story is going around, also how I threw up at Megan's party—that was the week after Katherine's visit. The story of the Columbia guy at Ping Pong Rocks has gotten quite spiced up, and a few of his friends have been thrown in.

I listen, nod, say things like, Hm, interesting. I tell myself, This is some other girl they are talking about. Not you.

Which is sort of true. And sort of not.

Ella says, "Then I heard—"

She bites her lip. I say, "God, Ella, don't stop now. I haven't gotten pregnant by aliens yet."

She laughs a little. Then tells me how the other day, Ramona Digby—"who, like, still hates you for some reason"—came up to her after history class and asked if what she'd heard was true.

What Ramona had heard was a story about me and David Potterich and his girlfriend, Amy, who goes to another school. And what we supposedly did at David's party over the summer.

"We were *joking*," I say. "It was a dare. Barely anything even happened."

"I know," says Ella unhappily. "That's what I told her. I was like, David's apartment is tiny. How would that even happen without the whole world seeing?"

"And?"

"She said someone told her they did see. Like, you and David and his girlfriend all kissing."

My face feels like it's in flames. "Yes, everybody got a kiss, that was it. David kissed me and Amy, I kissed David and Amy. Amy kissed us. Big whoop."

"Someone said it was making out."

"Well, that's a lie."

"I know, that's what I told her."

I tell myself, I don't care. I have nothing to be ashamed of. People can say what they want. I do not care.

After a moment, I remember to say, "Thanks for sticking up for me."

"God, sure."

"I can't believe people believe that."

"Well, you know who's telling them," says Ella.

Chloe, along with Isabelle and Zeena. Three little birds chirping their lies. Because, hey, the truth is so boring. Not to mention the truth doesn't make Chloe look so hot. *Yeah, I told my boyfriend I wanted to take a break—and can you believe it? He actually looked at another girl, oh, my God!*

"Just out of curiosity," I say, "what does Chloe have to say about me and Oliver?"

"Uh—that you hit on Oliver while she was in Europe. He was a little drunk and feeling lonely. You like, overwhelmed him or something."

"Uh-huh. So, they never had a fight, weren't taking a break."

"Chloe says they had made up." I can tell Ella is not enjoying repeating Chloe's version of events.

"And Oliver says . . ."

"Kind of . . . nothing."

That afternoon, I find a picture on my locker. A naked woman splayed out on a bed like a worn-out piece of meat.

Written across her, the word "SLUT."

There are two kids talking by the school news board. I look at them, but they just keep talking. They must have seen who did this. But they're pretending not to notice me.

Just then, Kevin Richmond comes through the door, laughing with his friend Andy Horowitz. Kevin and Andy are too dumb to pretend anything. They stop short at the sight of my locker. A huge grin comes over Kevin's face.

"Whoa," he says.

Andy jeers, "Somebody pissed somebody off."

I know for a fact Andy is not friends with Oliver or Chloe. Yet he's on their side. Why? Because I was dumb enough to make Chloe mad and now I can't handle the consequences. They are strong and I am weak. Nobody sides with the weak.

I rip down the picture, crush it in my fist, and throw it in the garbage. The two other kids look up from their talk. Kevin jokes, "Wait, I wanted that."

"Shut up!" I yell.

"Hey, don't piss off sluts, dude," says Andy. "Never know when you might need them."

"True," says Kevin. "Sorry, Tone. Hey, can I call you sometime? Like, do I have to come to you or do you make house calls?"

If I were smart, if I were strong, if I were the person I was before all this started, I would have an answer for Kevin. I would say, "Yeah, sure, but bring your credit card. I'm expensive." Or: "In your dreams." Or . . . something.

Instead, I burst into tears and run down the stairs.

Later, I realize my mistake. I shouldn't have thrown the poster away. I should have kept it as evidence. Gone to the administration.

But what are they going to do? Really? There's no proof Chloe did it. I can't see the school brushing for fingerprints. And the fact is, the school can't do anything. Maybe they could make sure I was okay while I was actually in school. But what about after?

And it's not just Chloe, it's everyone. That's what it feels like, anyway. It's like she's cast some spell over the whole school, turning them into zombies who go, *Attack, attack!* whenever they see me.

After school, Jackson Kinroth, Zeena's boyfriend, pulls at his pants and lifts his shirt up when I walk by. Licking his lips, he says, "I got five minutes before practice."

Over the weekend, the phone calls come.

"Is this the Hump Hotel?"

". . . the Freefux Motel?"

". . . the Eyelet Anyguy Inn?"

I stop answering.

"The thing to do," says Ella as we walk to school on Monday, "is not freak out. That'll just keep all this crap going."

That's why they're doing this? I think irritably. Because I'm freaking out? Why is everything about this my fault and none of it theirs? I stomp on the pavement. It's pissing rain this morning, big fat drops that explode on the sidewalk, splashing your legs with muck. I'm fighting to hold on to my umbrella, but I'm getting drenched anyway.

"Maybe you can talk to Chloe directly?" Ella raises her voice to be heard over the drum of the rain. "Without Isabelle and Zeena."

"Tried that," I yell. "Didn't work."

"What about Oliver? Make him be the prince who slays the fire-breathing Chloe and rescues you."

I shake my head; water drips from the edge of my umbrella into my eyes. "I think he wants to forget he ever knew me. Besides, I don't want to get Chloe more mad at me by going anywhere near him."

"Oh."

I sigh. The subject requires changing. I try to think beyond my own drama; what else is happening?

The only thing I can come up with is Cassandra. I ask, "How's your cousin doing?"

Ella pulls her umbrella closer. "I have no idea. Cassie and her parents came to brunch yesterday, and all anybody talked about was movies and the news. Oh—and my new diet and how it was going." She rolls her eyes. " 'Keep away from the bagels, dear.' "

"Yuck."

"Later, I found my mom and my aunt in the kitchen and it was obvious my aunt had been crying. The moment they saw me, they were like, It's fine, everything's fine, go away."

"Oh, man."

"Before they left, I said to Cassie, 'I'm really sorry, you must feel so sad.' She just looked at me like . . . Who are you? I wanted to scream at her, I know I'm not the brightest bulb in this family, but I am actually worried about you."

"She seems pretty tough," I say.

"You think so, yeah. But she takes things really hard. I mean, last spring break? She tried to kill herself."

"Excuse me?"

"Yah." Ella nods her head vigorously. "She fell madly in love with some college junior who was studying with her mom. And I think they had some kind of something, which is kinda cool, kinda mega-eww. But then he got the guilts about how young she was and broke it off. After which she slit her wrists. But, like, not the serious way."

"The serious way," I echo, disbelieving.

Ella holds out her wrist to show me. Drawing her finger down her arm, she explains, "If you cut with the vein, you're serious. Cut against it, you bleed a lot, but the slit isn't big enough for actual death."

"Aha."

"That's basically why I think she didn't really mean to do the deed. She just needed some drama for herself."

I glance over at Ella. I've never heard her be bitchy before. "What do you mean?"

"No, just in that family, it was all about Eamonn. It had to be. So I just wondered if she did it to get—" She shakes her head. "Never mind."

Maybe, I think, Cassandra really loved the guy. Maybe she wasn't okay with being played with and tossed away.

Maybe I do need to talk to Oliver.

* * *

Tuesday morning, I place Mimi in the calm, warm center of the windowsill. I move all the other figurines away from her. This is something she has to do on her own.

I take Dallas and place him near Mimi. To keep it real, I put him with his back to her.

Dallas the rabbit. Super shy, but somehow has his fun. That's good for Oliver.

In school land, Oliver is very into peace. Conflict resolution. Solving the world's problems. What I don't know is how good he is at these things in real life.

People believe Chloe's story of Oliver being drunk and confused when we hooked up because Chloe wants them to and people do what Chloe wants. But also because Oliver's an innocent. He doesn't quite get real life; it freaks him out.

They also believe it because Oliver isn't telling them anything different. Who knows, maybe he's even talked himself into believing that I'm some man-hungry beast who took advantage of him.

So I have to remind him otherwise—and get him to understand that you are not a nice guy if you let one person take the rap for something you both did.

At registration, I overheard Oliver setting up a special history tutorial with Mr. Greenaway for Monday lunchtime. So I have a pretty good idea of how to find him.

As I wait for Oliver to come out of Mr. Greenaway's office, I lean against the wall, rocking back and forth on my feet. I take deep breath after deep breath. When he appears, I want to be completely in control. I am not here because I like him. I am here because his girlfriend is being a bitch lunatic and it has to stop.

The door opens. I can see Oliver inside.

He says, "Okay, I'll work on that," to Mr. Greenaway, then shuts the door behind him. He keeps his gaze away from me.

He starts walking down the hall. I say, "Oliver."

Big exaggerated double take. "Oh, hey," he says, lifting a bony hand.

I try to see the boy who walked me home. The boy I liked.

I see Chloe Nachmias's scared, guilty boyfriend.

"How was registration?" he asks, keeping it safe. "Did you get the classes you wanted?"

"It went fine. Um—are you set for your Amnesty interview?" I hate myself for playing his game.

He nods anxiously. "It's next week. I was actually just talking to Mr. Greenaway about it. I really freeze up if I have to talk under pressure. Like I get all"—he makes *eee, eee* sounds. "So he gave me some vocal exercises."

I nod: Cool, whatever.

Then, slapping my hand against my book bag, I say, "Look, Oliver, I'm here because I need a favor."

He starts shifting from foot to foot. "What?"

"Chloe."

He shakes his head. "I don't think we should talk about—"

Desperate, I say, "I'm not here to bash her. You just need to tell her to back off. Okay? That's all I want."

He frowns. "What do you mean 'back off'?"

I feel a flash of annoyance: he doesn't even know what Chloe's been doing—or he doesn't want to know.

"I get that she's upset," I say carefully. "But she's been . . . letting me know she's upset. In kind of nasty ways."

What I want is shock, anger, an instant *I will deal with this, don't worry.*

What I get is suspicion.

"How do you mean 'nasty'?"

"Just . . . texts and phone calls. I mean, it's silly, yeah, but . . ."

He shakes his head. "Why would she do that?"

"I have no idea. But she's getting other people to do it too."

"Maybe it's her friends. . . ."

"Yes, them too. But also Chloe. They've been saying things about me. That are not true."

He looks away.

"I know you know what people are saying, Oliver."

"I don't really . . ."

He doesn't finish the sentence. I want to scream, What, Oliver? You don't really *what*? Don't know about it? Give me a break.

And then I get it. All this dirt about me has him thinking our nice little whatever was just my latest slutfest.

Planting my fists on my hips, I think, Okay, Oliver. You're right. It was all me. Our little fling had nothing to do with the fact that you're not so into your girlfriend but you are so into conflict avoidance you won't actually dump her. No, it's just that I'm a man-eating ho. So much easier for everyone if *that's* the truth. Well, not better for me, but who cares about that?

In the coldest voice I can manage, I say, "Tell her to stop, Oliver. Tell Chloe that you love her and her alone and she can forget about me. Okay?"

He thinks about this for a long time.

"I just think that'd be really tough," he admits. "I think it'd almost make it worse."

"It's not great now."

"Yeah, but if I stick up for you with Chloe, it's going to make her suspicious and pissed off."

He is really not going to do anything, I think numbly.

"But what she's doing is wrong," I try. "Because—"

"I don't think it's her," he interrupts. "People . . . talk. You know?"

Translation: When you slut around, people talk about you. This has nothing to do with Chloe, Toni. Nothing to do with me. It's all *your* fault.

"Um, hm," I say. "Okay. People talk. Guess what? I talk too. And here's what I have to say: You, my friend, are a gutless loser."

And I walk away.

I feel better for about five minutes.

Then the tears sting my eyes.

I hear people coming up the stairs. Loud chatter, the pounding of feet. Lunch is over. Everyone's back.

As kids pour into the hall, I turn around, pretend to stare at the school bulletin board. Chorus tryouts. French club. Amnesty International. Bake sale. Already, a bake sale. All these people just going on as if this stuff is really what school's all about. Happy, happy. Nothing's wrong! Nobody's mean! Here, have a brownie!

Who gives a shit, right?

The words are so clear, someone must have spoken. I spin around. But no one's standing behind me. I search the churning crowd for a familiar face, don't see one. But someone spoke to me, someone, like—read my mind.

Or something.

The crowd thins out. A few stray kids hang by the lockers, the water fountains. Only one stands by herself. Leaning against the wall in the exact spot I stood when I was waiting for Oliver.

Cassandra.

CHAPTER FIVE

"HEY," SHE SAYS AS I approach.

"Hi."

I can't help it. I glance at her hands. But the wrists are turned inward. If there are scars, I can't see them. She's standing by the window, the afternoon sun lighting her hair.

Now she says, "He totally blew you off, didn't he?" Her voice is brisk, matter-of-fact.

I look back, wondering if she saw my talk with Oliver. She couldn't have, I think. Nobody was here, I made sure. . . .

"I saw Oliver rushing down the stairs. Came here, saw you in tears. Not that hard to figure out."

For some reason, I laugh. No magic. Just thinking.

"You're Ella's friend," she says.

"Yup."

"Men suck. You know that, right?"

I smile. "Kinda learning."

"Not fun."

"No."

"Want to go somewhere?"

"Uh . . . sure."

Near the Riverside Playground on Eighty-Third Street, there's a rock pile. I used to climb on it all the time when I was a kid. The slope is vast and smooth. You look down on the playground; the children look tiny. Look down the other side and you see little benches, a gray path, the big stone wall that surrounds the park. When I was little, I would inch my sneakers up the gray stone of the rock, lift my arms, and pretend I was riding the back of a whale.

Now I'm sitting here with Cassandra Wolfe, of all people. My legs are pulled up, my arms locked around them. Cassandra sits cross-legged, her hair lifting off her forehead in the breeze.

She says, "So I hear you had a crazy summer too."

Eamonn. For a moment, I think, Does my dad and Oliver and everything else add up to . . . that? Not really. Still, I say, "I guess we could write some pretty dire 'What I Did on My Summer Vacation' essays."

"Whose horror story first?" she asks. "Yours or mine?"

"You already know mine."

Cassandra tilts her head to one side, recites, "Girl dares to have actual fun. Then she has actual fun with someone who is supposedly 'someone else's'—whatever that means. Girlfriend suddenly realizes she wants him back, so back he goes. *They're* all happy.

Other girl is branded slut by whole school for the sin of not being boring."

I smile. Cassandra's odd, theatrical way of talking is like a secret language; it makes me feel like we're in a club of tough, clever people.

She says, "You don't do the boyfriend thing, huh?"

"Not successfully."

She shrugs. "Maybe you don't want to. Maybe you don't care. I've noticed: you kind of float around. This guy, that guy." She raises an eyebrow. "I mean, really. What is that? Don't you know that as a female in high school your sole mission is to permanently attach yourself to a male in order to receive oxygen, sustenance, and social significance?"

"Crap, I knew I was forgetting something."

"You broke the rules," she scolds. "What were you thinking?"

"That I wanted to have some fun?"

"Bitch."

"I know, right?" I sigh. "So that's my horror story. What's yours?"

She rolls her eyes. But I notice she pulls her legs up, wraps her arms around them for protection. "I'm sure you've heard it."

I shake my head. Because I'm not one hundred percent sure which horror story we're talking about, boyfriend or brother.

"Hasn't Ella told you? It's one of her favorites." She looks out at the Hudson River. "So much excitement. So much fun. When it's not your pain."

I almost say, Yeah, Ella does talk about you—because she's worried about you. But Cassandra meets my eye, danger in her expression. This is not the time to defend Ella.

Then she shakes her head, as if annoyed with herself. "Zuh. Long story short: I fell madly, madly in love with a beautiful, dark-eyed lad who proved to be a lily-livered barstid. He dumped me, alas, alack. Having convinced myself that he was my own true love and read *Romeo and Juliet way* too many times, I tried to off myself."

She holds up her wrists. Now I see the scars, faint tracings on her skin. I imagine them open, bleeding.

"Can you believe that?" she says, dropping her arms. "How lame was I?"

"I don't think it's lame," I say truthfully. "It hurt. What's so great about pretending it didn't?"

"True," she agrees. "But really? My aim was way off. I should have slashed *his* wrists. Or his face. He was such a pretty boy." She sighs wistfully.

"Why didn't you?" I joke.

"Blinded by hormones? I don't know. No"—she gathers herself up—"I was a different person then."

"How'd you manage that?" I ask.

"Ah, I—"

Then she stops. Wrinkling her nose slightly, she looks toward the river.

"You what?" I prompt.

"That's a long story."

"I'm not going anywhere."

"No, it's—" She waves her hands in agitation—the first time I've seen her rattled. Almost to herself, she says, "How much craziness can I show you and not have you flee screaming?"

"Tell me."

She sits for a long moment, staring at my face.

"Not yet," she says finally.

Then she stands up. "Come on."

I get up. And follow.

Five blocks later I still have no idea where Cassandra and I are going. To Starbucks? The subway?

Cassandra, what is this?

She's walking a little ahead of me. I can see her brown hair as it bounces, her battered leather bag, her dark purple sweater.

Suddenly, she turns. "Sorry, I should've said. My house is right near. That okay?"

"Yeah," I say.

She stops. "I mean, if you want to talk about . . ."

"Yeah, I do."

She smiles. "Okay."

And now it hits me: I'm going to a place where a little boy died.

I stop. Cassandra says, "What?"

Uh, I can't go to your house, your brother just died.

Okay, how rude would that be?

"Nothing. Something I meant to tell my mom." I wave my arm forward. "Let's go."

Cassandra hesitates, like she knows exactly what I was thinking. Then nods.

We keep walking.

* * *

Cassandra lives on Central Park West. There is a doorman in a long coat and hat. He nods to Cassandra. She says, "Hey, Walter." I raise my hand, and Walter nods to me as if I've been coming here my whole life. I guess that's what people like doormen are for, to make you feel important.

"Nice guy," I say to Cassandra.

"Walter?" She smiles. "He knows all secrets."

"O-kay." I'm starting to figure out how to deal with Cassandra's mysterious statements: match her joking tone.

The lobby is a long, ornate cavern, like a hallway in some Russian mansion. Low benches covered in dark red velvet. Frosted glass keeping the light out. Tall claw-foot lamps glowing weakly. Mirrors everywhere you look. Mirrors on the wall, on the ceiling. You look up and there's your head floating in the air.

Laughter. A ripple of it, disappearing as suddenly as it came. I pause, not sure: did I hear that?

"What?" says Cassandra. A little impatient. I guess it's not the first time I've stopped.

"Uh, no." I shake my head. "I thought I heard something."

She takes me by the arm, pulls me toward the elevator. "Come on. You need tea."

In the silent hum of the elevator, I pull the sound from my memory. I did hear it. High, immediate laughter. Bright but thin. The sound comes from a skinny body, a young body . . .

A little boy's body.

We come out of the elevator onto the twelfth floor. Cassandra fishes in her pocket, pulls out a ring of keys, and opens the door.

What I'm most scared of? That one of her parents will be home and I'll have to say something.

"Don't worry," she says. "My parents are at work."

I don't know what I expected: The whole place draped in black? Organ music and wailing family members? But Cassandra's apartment is completely ordinary. Short hallway with a coat closet. Dining room table just as you come in. The galley kitchen beyond that. A sunken living room, that's the big thing you notice. And a lot of books lining the walls.

"Wow," I say. "Sunken living room. My mom would kill."

"It's a pain," she says. "You always trip. I'll make tea."

I'm about to say, Actually, I'm not a big tea person, but then I shut up. I don't have to drink, I can just sip.

Opposite the dining table there's a low, dark bureau. On top are family photos. My eye avoids, then finds Cassandra, then Eamonn.

He's skinny. With a big, cute-ugly clown grin. Curly hair.

"That's Eamonn." I jump, turn to see Cassandra behind me. "Well, obviously."

"He's cute," I say, to say something

"You think?" She sits down. "I guess. He's a little kid. What's not cute?"

She's brought out spoons for the tea. She taps one on the place mat. It makes a small, dull thud.

Trying to give her a chance to talk about it, I ask, "Does the place seem empty without him?"

There's a long pause. Cassandra stares hard at the table. "Honestly? It seems quiet. Did I mention I like quiet?"

The kettle shrieks. Cassandra goes into the kitchen and pours the boiling water into two cups. "You think that's sucky of me, right?" she says, bringing in the mugs. "To say I like quiet?"

"No." I take the mug. "Death seems way too complicated to have only appropriate feelings about."

"Yeah." She nods, but her face is closed. She sips her tea. I sip mine. Surprisingly, I like it.

She sees my surprise. "Yeah, it's different."

"It is." I sip again. Almost no flavor, but fresh like grass. Then a sourness.

"It's not actually something I want to talk about," says Cassandra abruptly. "I hope that's okay."

"No. No, that's—" I decide to borrow her word. "That's okay."

"Just it's . . . ah . . ." She looks away.

"You don't have to give it a neat little word," I tell her. "'Horrible' or whatever. I get it."

"Thank you." She nods, drinks her tea. Then she adds, "Although, we do seem to have this weird thing."

I laugh a little; it's hard keeping up with Cassandra. She's like a good basketball player, dodging left, right, faking you out all the time.

She says, "At certain times—I totally know what you're thinking."

"Yeah," I say after a moment. "I feel that way, too." Talking about the voice thing makes me feel shy for some reason.

"That first day at school? When you came up to me and were all 'I'm sorry'?" She laughs. "You were so pissed when I didn't react."

There's something about Cassandra's tone I'm not loving. I say, "I'm not sure it takes a mind meld to figure that out."

"'Screw you.' That's just what you were thinking. I knew."

"Yup."

"'I was just trying to be nice,'" Cassandra whines, mimicking me.

I feel slapped. Suddenly, I'm reminded that Cassandra doesn't have friends. Even Ella doesn't like her—and Ella likes everybody. When someone has no friends, there's usually a reason. This has all been a joke, a trick on Cassandra's part to get me here and insult me for some weird reason.

"Was I just a bitch?" Cassandra asks. Her voice is quiet, worried. Like she's coming out of an epileptic fit and she's not sure what she did.

"Kind of."

She nods. "I do that sometimes. Bad habit. Let me make it up to you."

She gets up and I feel how tall she is.

"Come on, I'll show you how I changed after Pretty Boy."

We go in the back of the apartment to Cassandra's room. It's dark, with the curtains closed. A fluffy dark red rug muffles our steps. The ceiling feels lower in here, though it could just be the gloom. The bed is unmade, with books and papers all over it. Most of one wall is taken up with bookshelves. It's a cave, I think.

This is what I thought it would feel like, I realize. In this whole apartment, Cassandra's room is the only one where you feel sadness.

Cassandra switches on a small light near her bed. A red-orange glow. I sit down on the bed. Cassandra goes to her closet.

I want to make a joke—vampires hating light, that kind of thing. But I'm getting a strong non-joke vibe. Cassandra is on her knees, her back to me, rummaging through her stuff. Then she stands. There's a notebook in her hand, her handwriting on the cover.

Crap, I think, I bet it's her poetry.

The book clasped to her chest, she says, "So. By any chance, have you ever cast a spell?"

It takes me a moment to understand. "Spell? As in magic?"

She nods, then sits down. "I don't mean Harry Potter, bibbity-bobbity-boo crap. I mean sending out your energy as an agent of change."

I nod deeply like I understand and take this seriously. "Aha."

"I mean, I was thinking. What have Chloe and her friends really done to you? They haven't hit you or beat you up."

"Yet."

"But they're making your life hell—and how? By making you a target. Using what? Psychic power. They've turned everyone's nasty, ugly, sneering energy beams toward you, like a thousand little ray guns. It's not an accident that there are three of them. Spells are way more powerful when you work with others."

She puts the book on the floor. "So I'd be happy to be your other. In honor of individual truth versus conformity."

Spells. Energy beams. I have an image of Chloe, Isabelle, and Zeena in witches' hats. Hesitant, I say, "Not so sure it's magic. I mean, you could just call it general bitchery."

She smiles, picks the book up off the floor. "Okay, we don't have to."

As she turns to put the book away, I blurt out, "No, wait—"

She turns back.

"What's the book?" I ask lamely.

The book hovers. "Ah—I can't show it to you if you're not into it. I'm not supposed to."

"Who says I'm not into it?"

She hesitates. "Just, it's not a joke."

"Sorry, I didn't mean to treat it as a joke."

"No, I know. But it won't work unless you take it somewhat seriously."

She sits down next to me on the floor. "Look—normally, I don't get this weird on a first date. But I feel like we have some kind of bond. I mean, yes, you got dicked over and I got dicked over. You had an evil summer, I did too. I feel like we're in the same psychic place. Which is really rare for me, because usually, my psychic space is not a place people want to be in, you know? Just not pretty."

She grins for a moment. Then stops, peers at me. "Did something else happen this summer? Not the parties. Something that hit your family, made you feel like the whole world was coming apart?"

Ella, I think immediately. She told Cassandra about my dad. My dad and Katherine.

Only—she couldn't have. Because I haven't told Ella.

"Maybe," I say carefully.

Cassandra nods. She already knew, I realize. Not the details, but that something happened. Because she's right: we are in the same psychic space. And it's not pretty. It's an ugly, spiky place where you feel sick to your stomach all the time. And I'm tired of being alone in there.

"I'm in," I say. Although I tell myself I only half mean it.

She smiles, prepares to open the book. "Antonia, meet my Book of Shadows. Book of Shadows, meet Antonia."

It's an incredibly thick book. The paper itself is heavy, almost like what you'd use for drawing. And it's stuffed with clippings and sketches and writing. As Cassandra flips through, I see that every page is covered with her scribbles.

We're sitting cross-legged on the floor. I peer into Cassandra's lap, but she's turning the pages too fast for me to really read anything.

"Traditionally, spell begging—or curse begging, which I assume you need—is frowned upon." She sees my confusion and explains, "Asking people versed in the occult to cast a spell for you."

She squints at the book, still searching for something. Leaving me to wonder, Is that what I'm doing? Asking her to cast a spell? On who? For what?

And, by the way, this is insane and I don't believe in this?

But I do understand what Cassandra said about sending out your energy. I remember Chloe and her friends surrounding me, suffocating me with their hate. That was some real nasty energy. And I wouldn't mind sending it back.

"So," says Cassandra. "I guess my first question is: who's the target?"

"How do you mean?"

"Who are we casting the spell on? It can't be a general 'go fuck yourself.'"

I point to the book. "That's not in there? Bummer."

"Just stronger if it's specific."

I think. Oliver. Chloe, Isabelle, Zeena. All those guys calling me for "appointments." I have a lot of people to hate.

"What happened this afternoon?" Cassandra asks. "Let's focus on that." She tugs on a loose thread on the cuff of my jeans. "Sorry, I'm a little OCD."

I think. My talk with Oliver seems so long ago now. "I was asking Oliver to talk to Chloe."

"So she'd quit with the evil energy."

I nod. "Or maybe just tell people that what she was saying about us wasn't exactly the whole truth and nothing but."

"And?"

"He acted like he didn't even believe she's doing it."

"So he's keeping his mouth shut."

"Yep."

"So he's a gutless barstid."

"Basically."

"What a jerk. You got some bad taste, lady."

"Blaming the victim," I joke.

"Don't *be* the victim," she says seriously. "So, sounds like Oliver's a good target."

I hesitate. I'm mad at Oliver, but I don't hate him. Not like I hate Chloe.

"You're thinking he's cute and it's Chloe who's the super-bitch," says Cassandra.

"Yeah," I say sheepishly. "Sort of. I mean, he's . . . nervous. Like, he has this big interview coming up and he's already freaking out. . . ."

"I got you." Her voice is easy. "It's always easier to blame the other chick. That's how guys get away with their crap."

Like Chloe blames me, while Oliver gets forgiven, I think. Cassandra has a point.

"But," Cassandra says cheerfully, "if you're not feeling in revenge mode, we can do a safety spell. See if we can get some protection going for you against Chloe."

"That sounds good."

Cassandra flips through the pages. "One Spell for Banishing a Demon coming right up."

Cassandra gets some incense out of her bureau drawer and lights it. It smells nasty, but she says it has to, to work. Then she opens the Book of Shadows.

"Repeat after me," she says. "Lofaham—"

"Lofaham." I try not to think how ridiculous the word sounds.

"Solomon—"

"Solomon."

As she chants and I answer, the incense grows heavier. I feel dizzy.

"Don't lose it," whispers Cassandra. "Stay focused. Really try to feel it."

And I try. I do. I try to gather my will, make it stronger than Chloe's. I try to feel the smoke is a fog, hiding me from Chloe's hatred. A shield against her anger.

But in my head, I know it's just cheap incense from Urban Outfitters. All it can do is give me a headache.

When we're done, Cassandra says, "I think it worked. I think I felt something."

"Yeah, I felt it, definitely."

But we're both lying. I didn't feel a thing and neither did she. And if we didn't feel it, it won't work.

My will is not stronger than Chloe's. She's angry; I'm afraid. Anger always wins over fear.

From beyond the door, we hear the click-clack of a lock turning. "Crapazoodie," says Cassandra. "That's my mom."

I stiffen.

"Don't sweat it," she says as she scrambles off the bed to put the Book of Shadows back in the closet. "She doesn't want to talk about it any more than you do. What she will almost certainly do is ask you—nay, beg you—to stay to dinner so that for once we have something to talk about. My advice: run for your life."

"I have my own awkward dinner to go to, unfortunately."

Cassandra laughs, her weird little bark that is the opposite of a giggle.

We hear "Cassandra? Honey?"

" 'Hey, Ms. Wolfe, nice to meet you,' " Cassandra instructs me in a whisper. "That's all you have to do."

She yanks the door open. "Hey, Mom!"

A woman comes around the corner, still in her coat and carrying a briefcase. She is little, with short, feathery hair and hard lines around her mouth. Next to her, Cassandra looks even more gargantuan. "Oh, hello," she says, seeing me. She looks up at Cassandra with an odd mix of . . .

Hope?

Fear?

"Mom," says Cassandra, "this is Antonia from school."

"Hi." Ms. Wolfe drops her briefcase on the floor, comes forward to shake my hand. I feel her eagerness like a big wet pink pillow about to slam into me.

"Hi, Ms. Wolfe. Nice to meet you."

Cassandra smiles.

"And now," says Cassandra, "Antonia from school has to go home."

"Oh." The pink pillow deflates, starts to sag. "She could certainly stay for dinner." She looks back at me. "You'd be absolutely welcome."

Her need is so huge, her pain so out there, it's like looking at a mirror that's shattered but still holding together—only just—a maze of jagged cracks on the verge of collapse. Saying no to her seems cruel. Glancing at Cassandra, I say, "Well, I could—"

"She's got her own awkward dinner to go to, Mom," says Cassandra, guiding me toward the front door.

As we hurry through the dining area to the entryway, Cassandra whispers, "First lesson: no mercy."

But your mom hasn't done anything to me, I want to say. She deserves mercy. From, like, the whole world.

"It won't help her," says Cassandra, "and it's a habit you need to break. Trust me. Bye, Antonia from school," she says loudly as she opens the door. "I'll think about that other thing."

"Cool," I say loudly, as if we're talking about homework.

The door closes. As I start for the elevator, I suddenly feel lost. The long corridor stretches before me with its unknowable doors and strange light. Where am I? I wonder for a moment. And where am I going?

Forward, I hear in my head.

So that's where I go.

"My goodness," says my mom as I come in the door. "We were starting to think you'd run off with the circus."

She is sitting at the dining room table, her laptop and a glass of wine in front of her.

My dad is in the kitchen. I hear the hiss of the frying pan, smell garlic and onion. The air in the apartment is thick with cooking—and something else. Something . . . not pleasant.

My dad appears at the kitchen window. "Table set?" he asks my mom.

She moves her eyes back to the screen in front of her. "Almost," she says.

I look at the table. It's a mess, covered with mail, my mom's papers, and old newspapers. Her coat hangs over a chair. There is nothing set here. My dad waits at the window, growing more frustrated with every second. My mom pretends not to notice, keeps typing. Every click of every key can be heard in the silence. I feel all this ugly emotion tangled like a mess of wire above our heads, sparking and hissing with dangerous energy. The longer my parents don't speak, the longer my mom refuses to look at my dad, the stronger that killer energy—the Katherine energy—gets.

I can set the table. The words form in my head, ready to be spoken. I imagine myself clearing the table, laying out the plates, chatting about this or that. My mom will talk to me; so will my dad. Eventually, they'll end up talking to each other. Katherine will fade out.

But then I remember what Cassandra said when I felt like I

needed to be nice to her mom: It won't help her, and it's a habit you need to break.

"Let me know when we're ready," I say, and go to my room.

Dropping my stuff on the floor, I lie on my bed. From outside, I hear the thud of a pot on the counter. My dad saying, "Claire?" and my mom, exasperated, "Yes, God, okay—"

They probably will get a divorce, I think calmly. My dad will move in with Katherine. In which case, I will definitely live with my mom.

Because even though she should have set the stupid table if she said she was going to? My dad shouldn't have cheated on her. And he shouldn't expect that everything's forgiven just because he said he was sorry. You let people down, you deserve to be punished. Because otherwise? Anyone can get away with anything.

My phone buzzes. I have a text. I look at the number. Ah, yes, Chloe.

A little bird tells me you talked to O today. That's a no-no. Punishment awaits.

Guess that protection spell didn't work out. No big surprise. Cassandra said you had to feel it. I didn't feel a thing.

I'm feeling it now, though. Quite strongly.

I text Cassandra:

I'm feeling revenge.

Maybe Cassandra's my prince, I think. Or wicked witch. Or whatever. I don't care at this point.

A moment later, I get a text back. *Meet me at the rock after school.*

CHAPTER SIX

CASSANDRA'S ALREADY THERE WHEN I get to the park. From the ground I can see her, perched high on the huge, smooth dome of the whale's back. She gestures, *Come up.*

"I've got it," she says happily as I collapse beside her. The book is in her lap.

"The spell?"

She nods. "So perfect. At first I was like, Hm, gutless, gutless, that's a good image. Got to be something there, some way to attack his insides. . . ."

"Puking his guts out?"

She nods approvingly. "Like that. Save it." She opens the book, turns it so I can see. "See what you think of this."

A SPELL FOR SILENCE

As I stare, the words seem to rise off the page. I feel hypnotized by them. Maybe it's that Cassandra has awesome handwriting. She's a total artist. But it's hard not to feel that the words alone have some kind of power.

Cassandra explains, "You know, 'cause he didn't speak up for you."

When I don't answer, she tugs the book back. "Okay, not working for you."

"No!" I grab the book. Then instantly let it go. I shouldn't be yanking her Book of Shadows around. "No, I love it. I'm . . ."

How to put this?

"What would it do to him?"

"Put him into a deadly coma from which he never awakes, thus ensuring his silence for eternity."

Her face is completely straight. Too straight.

I say, "Come on."

She laughs. "Sorry, had to. You looked so freaked. No, what it will do is make him unable to speak, but not hurt him. And we can do it light. Just for a day or two, if you want."

"How will it silence him?"

"Um, I believe the correct answer is . . . 'magic'?" She looks at me: Duh.

"No, I know, but it won't like, twist up his throat so he can't breathe, right?"

"Do you want it to?"

"Only every other Tuesday."

She grins, pleased that I got the joke this time. "No, this is a nonlethal spell. Technically, you're supposed to use it against other witches so they can't cast a spell on you. It's a defensive move. I just liked the imagery of it, since his silence cast a spell on you and did harm."

I like it too. I also like having Cassandra on my side, telling me that what people are doing to me is not cool. That I am not a skank.

I ask, "So how long, do you think?"

"How many days?"

I nod.

"Whatever you think is fitting."

I think. How many days have I been in hell? It's been almost a month since Chloe found out about me and Oliver. Thirty days. Is he responsible for all those phone calls and texts before school started?

No. But once it did, it's a different story. He might say he has no idea what Chloe's doing—but he does. School started two weeks ago—fourteen days. Should Oliver suffer in silence for that long?

Not, I tell myself, that I actually believe in any of this. But it'll make me feel better to do something.

Fourteen days is too long, I decide. Say this spell actually does something to Oliver's throat. Fourteen days of messing with your vocal cords has to do some damage. I don't want anything permanent.

On the other hand, I don't want anything trivial either.

When could Oliver be silent and it would really, really hurt him? But not forever.

Then I remember: his Amnesty interview. Four days from now. *I really freeze up if I have to talk under pressure.* Why not strike where he's weak?

I smile. "I think one week is sufficient."

Cassandra lifts the book to the sky. "One week be it."

The wind picks up, and the pages flutter like bird's wings.

* * *

You can't see it when you enter the park, but the rock has a large square cavern cut into it, almost as if the whale had a vast slice of blubber cut out of its side. Three sides are rock face, while the high wire fence to the playground faces you. Since there are trees and bushes planted on the playground side, no one can see what you're doing. It's the perfect place to drink, smoke weed—

Or do witchcraft. So that's where Cassandra and I go. Down into the pit.

We begin by finding a piece of rock. It has to be thin, although Cassandra won't tell me why. Finally, I find a sliver of dark shale.

"That'll work," says Cassandra.

We sit on the ground facing each other, the piece of shale in the middle. Then Cassandra reaches into her bag and takes out a small velvet pouch.

"How are you with blood?" she asks.

I have an immediate image of a slashed throat, blood gushing with every heartbeat. I shake it off.

"Um, define quantity."

Cassandra holds up a large needle. It's silver with a gold point. "A mere pinprick."

I hold out my finger. "Okay."

We arrange ourselves in a circle. "Okay," she says, wiping my finger with an alcohol swab. "I'm going to draw blood. When I do, your job is to write an 'O' on the stone."

"For 'Oliver.'" She nods. "Will it work with just an 'O'?"

"It's harder than you think to get blood." She smiles. "So, I think 'O' will have to do. Just keep him firmly fixed in your mind."

She takes my hand in hers, her skin hot with tension. Then she holds up the needle. "Don't look."

I turn my head, stare off into the trees. As I do, I let images of Oliver come into my head. Oliver laughing at the party, the feel of him against me on the street . . .

No, these are nice images. I want the real Oliver, the one I don't like.

Oliver not looking at me. Oliver with his dumb Uhhh. I don't know. I don't know. I don't know.

The stab of the needle hurts like hell. My hand jerks at the pain. Cassandra grips it tightly.

"Okay," she says. "Go."

My mind stuck on Oliver, confused by pain, it takes me a moment to remember what we're supposed to be doing. Then, with a dim memory of becoming blood sisters with Amy somebody at camp, I squeeze the tip of my finger until a bright red blood ball forms. I start to write on the slab.

The first touch is too much. It leaves a clumsy crimson blotch on the stone, which soaks in.

"More," says Cassandra.

I squeeze harder, drawing the tip of my finger along the stone. A thin line begins to form.

"Keep going," she urges. "Think of him. Think of what he did. How he let you down."

I do, pressing harder and harder until it feels like I'm going to crack my nail.

"Here." Cassandra grabs my hand, stabs my finger again. I barely feel it, desperate to have enough to complete the circle. I start feeling light-headed, as if it's gallons I'm pumping instead of droplets. It's so slow, takes so long.

Weak, I think, don't be weak. You can do this, you can.

When the two red swoops finally join at the splotch, I burst out laughing with happiness.

"Perfect," says Cassandra.

Panting, I say, "The blotch isn't so great."

"No," she says, her voice distant. "It's the primal wound. The first hurt he gave you that started the circle of cruelty. Now you've brought it all back to him."

"That's right," I say.

Cassandra takes a deep breath. "Before we go on, I do have to tell you one thing."

"Okay."

"The Threefold Law. Or the Law of Return, whichever you prefer," she says, going back to her jokey voice. "Basically it says whatever energy you put out, you get back. Times three."

"So, if I make Oliver silent for a week, I could be silent for three weeks."

She nods. "Or—lose another sense. Your hearing, your sight."

"In other words, karma's a bitch."

"Precisely. Now—do you want to know why I think that won't happen?"

"Please."

"I think it won't happen because the Threefold Law has already been set in motion. We're making it happen right now. If you do this, you even the score. But that's just what I think," she adds uncertainly. "I don't want to talk you into it."

"What's the worst that can happen?" I ask. "So I won't be able to smell or whatever for a week."

"You're sure?"

I nod. "What's next?"

Cassandra picks up her bag, draws out a nail and hammer. Something is tied around the nail. Two somethings—a small crimson thread and a blue thread, intertwined.

"I took the red thread from Oliver's backpack," she explains. "And I took the blue thread from your jeans when you came over."

I remember Cassandra tugging, her little joke about OCD. "Just had a feeling you'd be needing it."

She smiles. "Kind of. So, what you do is take this hammer and pound this nail through the 'O.' It fixes the spell in place."

"Like a stake through the vampire's heart."

"Probably the same reasoning. I'll say the words for the spell. And when I'm done, you do your thing."

I take the nail, place it in the center of the "O."

Cassandra asks, "Are you ready?"

I nod. She hands me the hammer. "I'm going to start now," she tells me. "Whatever you do, do not interrupt."

"Okay."

Then she closes her eyes. "I call thee spirit, cruel spirit, merciless spirit . . ."

Cruel? Merciless? I open my mouth.

DON'T interrupt, I hear in my head.

"I call thee, bad spirit, who takes away healing from man. Go and place a knot in O's throat. In his tongue and his windpipe. Let the knots grow and swell for seven days. Then at the end of seven days, let them be no more. Because I wish it. Amen. Amen. Selah."

She opens her eyes, looks at me. My turn.

I place the point of the nail in the middle of the "O." Raise the hammer high. Then I bring it down hard on the head of the nail.

It goes through cleanly. Not a single crack.

Cassandra smiles. "Good."

We bury the stone and the nail in the ground. I press the hill of earth smooth with my shoe, feel as if I'm stepping on a grave. This time the spell feels much more real than the safety thing we tried in Cassandra's room. I'm exhausted, like I really did send some serious energy out to Oliver.

The sun is going down, casting flares and shadows around us. The cavern is cold. I remember that the park changes after dark. The creeps come out.

"Are you okay?" Cassandra asks. "It's intense."

"It is. But I think I'm all right. What do we do now?"

"Now? We wait. Oh—and I was thinking?"

I nod.

"Maybe it's best if we don't hang out so much at school."

My heart lurches. The sucky thing about being rejected is you start to expect it all the time. "Why?"

Cassandra sighs. "Just, with Ella—I know you two are friends, and I know she can be sweet. But she needs other people's lives to feed off, you know? I'm not saying she's a parasite." She shakes her head. "There I go again, bitch alert. Just . . . cousins get competitive. Our moms compare us, and it's a drag. I'm sure Ella gets sick of hearing about my grades, sports, whatever. So, I don't want the added drama of 'You stole my bestie!' You know what I'm saying?"

Remembering Ella's comments about Cassandra, I can understand what Cassandra means. "I get you."

"Also, if this works?" She nods back toward the rock. "We don't want people asking questions. You know, it helped that I could get near Oliver's stuff without him connecting me to you."

I nod. Then think, What kind of questions could people ask? What have we actually done?

The next day, I walk with Ella to school. As she chatters on about this and that, I barely hear her. All I can think is Is it today? Will it happen today?

What if Cassandra's toying with me? Playing one of her not-so-funny jokes? *Oh, my God, you actually believed me? How sad are you?*

Or—what if something truly awful happens to Oliver?

Two cars at the corner: Con Ed and a bakery van. If the bakery van moves first, Oliver will be fine. If it's Con Ed, he'll be seriously effed up.

The bakery van moves first. I feel an odd sense of relief.

Only I hope that doesn't mean *nothing* will happen to him.

When we get to school, I look for some sign of catastrophe. On the stairwell, in the hall, I strain to listen in on conversations, expecting to hear

Oliver fell down a flight of stairs and broke his neck!

Oliver's cat scratched him and cut a vein in his throat and he bled to death!

Oliver choked on a walnut and died!

But it's all homework and TV and who said what to who on Facebook. It seems there has been no great tragedy involving Oliver.

Ella asks, "Why are you staring at everyone?"

I blush. "No, nothing."

Stella Eberly walks past us. I smile hi. Stella used to smile back. But not today. Not since I've become the school tramp.

Stupid, Toni, I think as I head to homeroom. Stupid, stupid Toni. Nothing has happened. You have no power. Today will be just another day of Slam the Slut.

Why did I ever believe Cassandra?

Then I see Chloe, Zeena, and Isabelle standing by the water fountain. I stop, try to feel their vibe. Chloe is not crying or hysterical—which she certainly would be if Oliver's cat had slashed his jugular and he was dead.

But she definitely seems . . . worried. For one thing, she hasn't even noticed I'm here.

Inching closer, I hear Chloe say, "Yeah, he texted me saying he wasn't sure what was wrong. . . ."

I stop dead, not caring if Chloe sees me. Something is wrong with Oliver. Actually, really wrong. Which means . . .

Which means the spell worked.

I did it. I have power.

Then Zeena sees me, nudges Chloe in warning. Chloe looks and snarls, "*What?*"

"She just wants to know about Oliver," Zeena sneers.

"Sluts have no self-control," adds Isabelle.

In real rage, Chloe swings her fist backward; it slams into a locker. She screams, "This is none of your business. Get away—or I will *hurt* you!"

My body is obedient, I start walking. But this time it's different. This time, I keep my eyes on Chloe. This time, I'm not afraid. When Chloe said she'd hurt me, what I thought was *And I'll hurt you back.*

* * *

At lunchtime, Ella and I go to Nuts for Soup. As we walk down Eighty-First Street, Ella says excitedly, "Did you hear what happened to Oliver?"

I pretend to have to think about it. "Something with his voice?"

"Yeah!" Ella's eyes widen and she leans forward. "He totally cannot talk. It started last night and they have no idea why."

"Wow," I say in a bored voice.

"And he's freaking out because his big interview thing is in a few days."

"Gee." I reach in my bag and check my phone. As I do, I can feel Ella watching me closely.

"I'm registering total noninterest here," she says, puzzled.

"You register right," I tell her.

She looks doubtful, but says, "Well, hey, good for you."

I nod as if I couldn't care less. But it's hard not to punch the air and shriek, "Yes!" I asked the spirits to take away Oliver's voice— and they did. I wanted him to miss his Amnesty interview—and he will.

It's amazing. It's . . . magic.

Ella says, "Would it be okay if we ditched the soup? I could kill for a cheeseburger."

There even seems to be less slut baiting today. Either Chloe's all worried about Oliver so she forgot to send out the daily torture memo—"Everyone eat bananas in front of her at lunch— slowly!"—or maybe I don't come off as such a victim anymore.

After school, I see Cassandra as I leave the building. She's leaning against a truck, reading *The Crucible*. As I approach, she smiles.

We head for the park.

* * *

"So . . . ," I say carefully after a few blocks, "looks like things are working out."

"I have no idea," she says blankly. "Let's find out."

We climb to the top of the rock. From up here, we can see little kids on the playground. One pushes another off the swing and she cries, runs to her mom. The other kid just takes the swing.

Cassandra crosses her legs, says, "Okay."

"Okay what?"

"Call him," she says simply.

I dig my phone out of my bag. "Going to be a little weird if I call and Oliver can't speak."

"That's the final proof that it worked."

I nod. Punching Oliver's number, I feel Cassandra, excited and expectant, next to me. That hum.

I can't wait!

I know, me too!

"Ringing," I whisper.

She squeezes my wrist.

"Hello?"

A man's voice. It's a nice voice, slow, a little tired. Oliver's dad.

"Hi," I say. "My name's Toni. I'm a friend of Oliver's."

"Oh." Hesitation. Worry. I can hear it. It thrills me.

"He wasn't at school today, so I wanted to call. See if he's okay."

From Cassandra, a surge of pleasure. I am lying so well.

"Ah, well, I'm afraid Oliver's not—" He interrupts himself. "He's fine. He will be fine."

"Can I talk to him?"

89

"No, that's what I was going to say. I'm afraid you can't. Oliver's having a little trouble with his voice."

I have no idea what heroin feels like, but I can't imagine it's better than the rush that courses through me at that moment. I feel in complete control of the entire universe. I know everything worth knowing. I am untouchable, but no one is beyond my power. I reach out, find Cassandra's hand. Our fingers curl around one another, the rings of our palms sealed together.

"Oh, man," I say sympathetically.

"Yeah, the doctors aren't sure what it is." I grin, all teeth. "They feel it's stress related and almost certainly not permanent. But obviously, it's very upsetting."

"Sure."

"So I'm afraid he can't talk to you. I'll tell him you called, though."

"No, don't bother," I say. "I'll see him in school. Let the poor guy rest his vocal cords." I raise my eyebrows at Cassandra, who grins maniacally. "I hope he's taking it easy," I add.

Oliver's dad says, "Well, of course he's very worried that he might miss the interview on Monday."

Might. Something horrible occurs to me: What if they can just reschedule it and all of this has been for nothing?

I say, "Well, they'll set up another one, right?"

"Uh, not really. If he's not better soon, Oliver has to give his slot to someone else."

"Oh, no," I sigh.

"Yes, it's a bad thing."

"Tell him I'm sorry," I manage to say before hanging up.

I toss the phone down and we scream as one, a long shriek of

total happiness. Seizing each other's hands, we dance, hips sway-
ing, feet twitching, singing, "Da, da, da...," like we're doing
some crazy cha-cha. Cassandra spins me under her arm. I spin her.
We dance back-to-back, hands joined. I sing to the sky, "We did
it! We did it!"

As we leave the park, I say, "Have you ever done that before?
Like—had it work?"

Cassandra hesitates. "Not like that," she says finally. "Not
as well."

I want so badly for her to tell me what she tried before, how
it didn't work, how I helped her make it work. But I can tell she's
not up for revealing right now.

"We could try it again," I suggest. "I mean, hey, you helped me.
Your turn now."

She smiles. "Nah, nothing I need right now."

"Okay," I say. "But I owe you."

Cassandra says, "I'll remember that."

CHAPTER SEVEN

IT'S LATE BY THE TIME I get home. As I come through the door, I hear my mom say, "Here she is, Henry—" and my dad say, "Ah, thank God!"

"What?" I say, looking at both of them.

"The game," says my mom brightly, with only a hint of sarcasm. "The big, big game!"

"Oh, right." Game night. Thursday nights, we get takeout and watch a basketball game. One of our very few family traditions. I was so excited about the Oliver spell, I forgot today was game night.

Now my dad's looking at me anxiously. My mom's clearly ready to blow off our Thursday-night ritual. Am I going to join her and refuse to participate in family stuff, to show him how he wrecked everything?

Another time, I might have. But I feel like the universe was very generous to me today, and I want to be generous back. So I say, "Cool! Who's playing?"

"The Mavs versus the Lakers." My dad lowers his voice and narrows his eyes as he says "the Lakers."

My parents do not root for winners. Because we live in New York, they root for the Knicks. But they'll give their heart to any team that has a lot of old players looking for a title, so-so players that don't get a lot of press, and little guys that try hard. My dad hates L.A. with a passion. My mom detests Miami. If you're powerful, arrogant, and win a lot, you won't have my parents as fans. I bet LeBron James is very sad about that.

So tonight, we abandon the kitchen and the dining room table and move to the living room. My dad sits on the couch, my mom takes an armchair. I kneel on the floor so I can put my dinner on the coffee table. As we eat Chinese food and watch Dallas versus L.A., we are united. Every time Kobe Bryant goes for a shot, my mother points two fingers at the TV and makes a *zzzt, zzzt* noise to put a hex on him.

Kobe's making free throws. My mom says, "*Zzzt, zzzt . . .*"

I say, "Ma, seriously."

Kobe misses. "See?" says my mom. "*Zzzt, zzzt.*"

He makes the next shot.

"It's hard to get the hex all the way cross-country," she says.

"Sure, Ma."

My dad is smiling, amused by our back-and-forth. This is turning out to be a good night for us. The game fills in the silence. We can put our evil thoughts onto guys we've never met and know that the worst thing that can happen is someone loses.

My dad loves Dirk Nowitzki and Jason Terry. Not only are they old, but six years ago, when they had their best shot at winning, they lost in the finals and the other team celebrated on their court. This level of loserdom and humiliation earned them my dad's loyalty for life, even though they did win a championship last year.

Dirk goes to the foul line. My dad leans forward. He gets super intense about foul shots. I guess because it feels like they happen in slow motion, it's like the whole victory/defeat drama plays out over a minute.

Dirk crouches. Shoots. Misses.

"They could have used that point," my dad mutters.

"He'll make the next one," I say.

But Dirk misses that one, too. My dad settles back in his chair. My mom glances at him.

The Mavericks play badly. Missed shots. Lots of turnovers. L.A. takes a serious lead. My mom starts getting restless.

My dad looks up. "What?"

"No—I'm just thinking about some things I promised to do. . . ." She waves her hand. "Never mind."

My dad keeps looking at her, even when she goes back to staring at the screen.

I watch the game. Dallas has come back a little bit. But there's only three minutes left to play. If they're going to win, they're going to have to make every shot.

My dad says to me, "Remember when you were little? You'd stand on one foot as a good-luck thing?"

"Oh, yeah." I smile, pleased that his head is in the happy past instead of the weird present.

Wanting to keep it there, I stand up, lift one leg. "You watch, Terry's going to make this shot."

"Uh-huh," says my mom skeptically.

"You watch," I say. "I have magic powers."

I try to believe that as I wobble on my one foot. In my head, I chant, Make the shot, make the shot, make the shot. Then, You win, we win. You win, we win. I'm not even sure what that means, but it feels like it's coming from that place where the spells start to grow.

Terry lifts up, makes the shot. My dad crows, "Hey!" All of a sudden, there's energy in the room again.

Scrambling back to my seat, I say to my mom, "Told you."

"You did."

"Here comes Barea," says my dad. Barea is the Mavs' little guy. Practically my height.

"He should pass," says my mom worriedly.

"Foot, foot." My dad points at me.

I get up, stand on the one foot. Think only, You win, we win. You win, we win.

"And he makes the shot from downtown!" cheers my dad.

"Whoo!" I call from my perch.

Before I can go back to my seat, L.A. turns the ball over and Dallas makes another two points. "Stay there, stay there," says my dad.

"They need you," jokes my mom.

The Mavs are winning and that awful feeling of flatness and defeat has left the room. You win, we win, you win, we win. . . . I chant it over and over, my leg bent at the knee. You win, we win, you win, we win. My eyes are closed now, despite the fact that it's very hard to stay on one foot that way. I hear my parents cheering, "Go, go, go!" A burst of "Oh, yeah!" and clapping.

My mom counts down the clock, "Ten, nine, eight, seven . . ."

And the game is over. The Mavs have won. And my parents

are with me on my one foot and we're all ridiculously bunched together and hugging.

On Tuesday, I'm in the library when I overhear Jacob Carpio talking to Lily Bar David. "Yeah, I talked to his dad yesterday. He had to skip the interview."

Jacob and Lily are friends with Oliver. They must be talking about him, they have to be. I slip behind a bookcase so they don't see me.

Lily says, "Poor guy, he must be so bummed."

"Pretty much," says Jacob. "Let's face it, this hasn't been the best year for him. . . ."

There's a short silence. Then Lily asks, "Has he seen Chloe at all?"

"I don't think so."

"Hm," says Lily. "Well, maybe that's not the worst thing."

"Maybe not," says Jacob.

Well, I think. Well, well, well.

The next day, I'm cramming stuff into my locker when Ella hurries over and asks, "Do you want to hear Oliver-and-Chloe gossip or you don't care?"

"Eh," I say casually. "I'm easy. Hit me."

She beams. "Well, you know how he lost his voice and couldn't do the interview?"

I nod.

"Apparently, he's in mondo depression mode. His friends are

all visiting him, trying to cheer him up. Only there's one friend he doesn't want to see. . . ."

She pauses for dramatic effect. "Wanna guess who?"

"Does it start with a 'C'?"

"Wild, huh? And she is de*mented*."

I shrug. "What else is new?"

Just then, Cassandra comes out of the stairwell. I remember she asked me not to let Ella know we're friends, but it's impossible. She's right there in front of us.

As casually as I can, I say, "Hey."

Cassandra nods, says "Hi" to the space between me and Ella. Then she keeps walking down the hall.

I feel Ella looking at me. She says, "I didn't know you guys knew each other."

"Because of you," I mumble, and wonder why I feel like I'm cheating.

On Friday, I'm on my way out to lunch when I spot Chloe on the plaza outside the entrance to school. She's on the phone, pacing one step forward, one step back as she listens. I hang back, out of immediate sight range.

Chloe's nodding impatiently.

Finally, she interrupts. "I promise, I swear, I will not make him talk for long, Mr. Chen. Just—if his voice is getting better . . ."

It's been one week since Oliver lost his voice. He should be able to talk now. There's a pause. Then Chloe snaps, "Well, I know he talked to his friend Jacob, so I know he *can* talk."

So Oliver hasn't even called Chloe.

Softer now, she says, "I understand. I guess, let him know I'd love to hear from him? Okay. Thanks, Mr. Chen."

As I duck back inside school for safety, I think, Gee, Chloe. First your man cheats on you, then he has a major crisis and doesn't get in touch. . . . Kind of unsettling. I could almost feel sorry for you.

Almost.

I look up, see Cassandra come out of the stairwell. She pauses to look at the school announcement board, a sign she doesn't want to make contact.

But she puts her hand behind her back, wiggles her fingers at me.

I wiggle mine back.

Monday. The interviews are over. The committee has left. And Oliver is back at school.

I tell myself this is not important to me. What is important is studying for my first Spanish test. Thank God, I have a free study period in the morning. On the second floor, there's a row of study cubbies—basically a long desk with little walls set up to create white boxes. Most of them have tiny graffiti notes on the walls.

As I sit down at one, I see a little tiny scribble. It says, "Ban all sluts!"

I lick my thumb, try to rub it out. It leaves an ugly blue smear. I get up and move.

Then I hear, "Hey."

Oliver is standing by my seat.

"Hi." I keep it neutral. "How are you?"

"Okay." His voice is still thin and scratchy. "My dad said you called. When I was—" He looks down, seems in fact to lose the power of speech.

I can't resist. "Did the doctors say what it was?"

He nods. "They said stress. That maybe the whole thing with the interview—like, I put too much pressure on myself and my body had this weird reaction."

"Oh."

"They said maybe it was just as well I didn't get the internship. That I need to learn to take it easy. I've been thinking a lot about that. How hard I take stuff. I have to not do that." He actually looks me in the eye to say this: "Not blame myself for every little thing."

Wow, I think. Medical permission to be a jerk. Nice.

"Well, glad you're better," I say, and turn back to my work.

Oliver perches on the edge of the next seat over, says, "Just— when I was sick? When I couldn't talk? I kept thinking—"

He strangles on his own words. I say, "Yeah?"

"I don't know. I had this huge feeling that there was something I needed to say to you. When my dad said you called, I somehow felt like you knew that. I know that sounds totally insane."

Not entirely, I think. "What'd you feel like you had to say?"

He sighs, stares into the white cube like it has answers. "Just . . . you've been nice to me. With everything that happened, you could have been harsh, but you weren't. Like, you even called to see how I was doing. That was really cool."

This makes me feel slightly guilty. "Well . . ."

Oliver takes this as an apology. Nodding eagerly, he says, "I mean, maybe you were a *little* harsh that one time when you were upset about Chloe—"

Upset, I think. Is that what I was? How about totally freaking out?

Then Oliver says, "But I get why that happened."

This is meant to be a big fat gift. Oliver "gets it." Only he so doesn't. I feel a surge of anger and I look down at the floor. The hate is running through my body like an electric current.

Even Oliver clues in. He stammers, "Well, anyway, I—I . . ."

My head snaps up. "What, Oliver? *What?*"

His lips move, but nothing comes out. Guess the curse is still working.

But then he blurts out, "I miss you. I'd really like us to be . . ."

At this point, I don't care what Oliver wants.

I'm about to shove back my chair and get up. Then I see Zeena standing at the door to the computer lab. Oliver half rises in a panic. From Zeena's expression, there's no question that she heard what he said.

Oliver blithers, "Uh, oh, hey, Zeena . . ."

Zeena's hostile eyes are fixed on me. She advances, saying, "Don't . . . even . . . think . . ."

But you have to have some wit to finish that sentence, and Zeena has none. Pushing back my chair, I say, "Excuse me. I think this is my cue to split."

As I go, I hear Zeena call, "Yeah, you better run. Run fast. But don't think we won't find you. Don't even think—"

I wave my fingers in the air à la Cassandra. Over my shoulder, I say, "Ciao, Oliver. Nice talking to you."

* * *

That afternoon, Ella rushes up to me. She's all excited and pop-eyed. I swear, I can feel her vibe like a million tiny tentacles reaching out to suck up other people's energy.

"Hey!" she says, breathless. "Are you okay?"

"Sure, yeah. Why?"

"Uh, um . . ." Ella bobs like a beach ball. Then she cries, "Zeena's telling the whole world she saw you and Oliver together. Like *together* together."

"Oh, for—"

"Is it true?"

"*No*, it's not true. We talked for like a minute."

She bites her lip. "Well, you might want to let Chloe know that. Zeena said you guys were flirting big-time. Chloe's totally on the rampage."

And of course she's blaming me. My stomach tightens.

"Are you okay?" Ella asks. *Are you freaking? Can I see? Can I see?*

"I'm fine," I bark.

"Okay." She nods uncertainly. "Only—"

"What?"

"Just—I was going to ask if you want to walk home today."

I'm so scared and furious, I can't think. I sputter, "I don't know when I'm leaving."

Ella hesitates. "I think you should really go straight home. And someone should be with you. Chloe's really, really mad."

"Chick is de*ranged*," I say, my voice rising.

"That's what I'm saying," says Ella. "I'm worried she's going to try and . . . do something to you. Do you want me to walk you home?"

Ella is a sweetheart. But I don't need a sweetheart right now. I need Cassandra. She and I are a team; together we have the power.

"No," I tell Ella. "I'll be fine."

CHAPTER EIGHT

ALL AFTERNOON, I SEND OUT distress signals to Cassandra.

Hello, Cassandra?

Yo, babe, need you.

Seriously. Kind of in trouble here.

I get back silence. Come to think of it, I haven't seen her today. What if she's not even in school?

I can feel the eyes on me all afternoon.

Everyone knows. Everyone knows.

I have my Spanish test last period. I can't concentrate. When I finish, I take my paper up to Señorita Romero. I glance at the clock: three-twelve. Usually by three-thirty, the only people left in the building are kids doing after-school stuff.

Oh, and the ones who are waiting to kill you.

Cassandra, please!

Three-fifteen. School's over. Kids tumble out of class, racing for freedom. I try to stay with the crowd as much as possible.

In the hallway, I run into Malcolm Willander, who asks if I

understood what we were supposed to do for calc. He is half flirting with me, and even though I'm not into him, I wonder if it's worth it to keep the conversation going for protection.

Then two of his friends come by. He says, "So, catch you later?" and I say, "Yeah, text me," and we're done.

Three-twenty-five. There are still some kids lingering. If I hurry—but not obviously—and stick to crowded areas, I can make it out of the building.

I bump into Nina Watts, who's on her way to drama club. Wagging a finger, she says, "Were you talking to Oliver, naughty girl?"

"Not me," I throw over my shoulder, and keep going.

I pull open the door to the stairwell, look down it. The dark tunnel feels scary.

Most kids are gone now. If I get stuck in an isolated spot, I could be dead. Maybe I should just wait this out. Stay put till everyone's gone. Chloe and Co. won't wait around forever. I'm sure they have some tremendously important shopping to do.

I turn around, head back toward the library. There's always someone in the library after school—some club or kids doing work. And even if no one's there, books just feel safe. You can't hurt someone around all those books, right? If I can just make it to the library, I'll be safe, I think crazily, now all but running down the deserted hallway.

"Finally," says Chloe, stepping out in front of me. Startled, I gasp.

I turn to run, but Zeena and Isabelle move in behind, blocking my exit.

"Hold her," says Chloe. Zeena's nails dig into one wrist, Isabelle's into my arm. They start shoving me toward a nearby bathroom. I wriggle, squirm, try to flail free. But they're too strong, too fast.

Chloe opens the bathroom door—"Madame," she says with a nasty smile. And I am pushed inside.

Our school bathrooms have three stalls with doors. To the left are three sinks and a long mirror. All the stalls are empty. I take a deep breath, get ready to scream for help. Suddenly, I feel an explosion of pain at the back of my skull. Someone's got my hair in her fist and is twisting hard. I cry out, swing my backpack, desperate to hit her. Zeena catches my hand and claws my fingers off the strap. Then she tosses the bag to Isabelle. I hear a splash and laughter. I am vaguely aware that my backpack is now in the toilet.

My hand hurts so fucking bad, worse than anything. There is blood. I can feel it sticky on my fingers.

"That's it for the bag," says Chloe lightly. "Now for the bitch."

A wrestling match. Isabelle and Zeena take hold of my arms, start dragging me back. Instinctively, I struggle, twisting my body around, flinging myself forward. Chloe reaches down, grabs my ankle. I kick wildly, but Isabelle and Zeena pull me back and I end up on the floor. They drag me by the arms into the stall. I drum my feet on the floor, make horrible whining noises, but I don't have the breath to really scream.

My head is slammed against the porcelain rim and I go into a whole new place of pain.

Zeena giggles. "Oops."

"Let's see if hair flushes," says Chloe.

My hair is gathered and yanked so hard, my head lifts up; now it's my neck on the rim of the toilet. I smell something bitter, suffocating.

"Oh, Zeena," tuts Chloe, "you didn't flush."

"Bad me," says Zeena.

There's shit in my hair, I think with odd detachment. I'll cut it off when I get home. I feel the piss water seep into my hair, my head grows heavy. It's getting harder to breathe, my neck is at such a weird angle. Not a good way to die, actually, strangling in the toilet.

"Clean rinse," says Chloe.

I hear Isabelle say, "Guys?" She sounds nervous, and for a moment, I have hope.

But then I am flopped over. The wind is knocked out of me as my chest slams against the rim. Toilet stink hits my nostrils just before my face is slammed into the water. Something solid brushes my cheek and I gag hard.

Zeena drops the seat over my head. Pretends to sit on it.

They're going to drown me. On purpose or by accident. I can't breathe, this is bad, I can't breathe, I can't breathe!

Only when Zeena stands up do I realize I've been screaming this out loud. I thrash away from the toilet, crying. My wet hair spatters piss water all over me.

And they're laughing. Chloe and Zeena are laughing so hard they have to hold on to the sinks to stand up. Isabelle is by the door, a strange, frozen smile on her face. Their ugly, hateful spirits slam at my consciousness and all I can process is Hate you. Destroy you.

And then the door whines as it opens, thuds closed. Silence.

They're gone. It's over.

I start to cry again.

I don't really know for how long.

Then the door opens again. Cassandra comes through, humming her odd tune. From the floor, I see her frown; maybe the smell reached her. She looks down. Sees me.

"Oh, my God." She kneels down beside me. I feel her touching my face.

"What happened? Are you okay?"

I nod and shake my head at the same time.

"Duh, no, obviously," says Cassandra. "Can you stand up?"

"I don't think so."

"I'll get you a cloth," says Cassandra, standing.

A few moments later, cool wetness on my cheek. The hot stickiness of tears and the bitter stain of piss is wiped away. I take a deep breath.

Cassandra says matter-of-factly, "This was Chloe, right?"

Just the mention of Chloe's name feels humiliating. I tear up again, nod.

Then, in my head, *Stop it. Quit crying. Crying doesn't help you.*

I look up at Cassandra. Her face is still, watchful. She doesn't feel the least bit sorry for me, I realize.

Waste of time.

"I guess there's no point in just sitting here."

"Not really," she says.

"Maybe I'll stand up."

"Good idea," she says.

There are showers at our school, but they're far away, and I'm not walking through the halls like this.

Cassandra helps me wash my hair in the sink with soap from the dispenser. I take off all my clothes, scrub myself with harsh paper towels.

At one point, a teacher tries to come in. Cassandra blocks the door without fuss, calling, "Period crisis. Privacy necessary."

I tell Cassandra my locker combination, tell her what to look for. She comes back carrying my gym shorts and sweatshirt. I put them on. My sweater and jeans I wrap into a tight ball.

"I have a bag you could put those in," says Cassandra, wrinkling her nose slightly.

"Nah," I say, and dump it into a garbage can on our way out of the bathroom. I am never wearing those clothes again.

I must look strange in my shorts and coat, but I don't care.

"Where do you want to go?" Cassandra asks as we leave the building. It's four-thirty. Amazingly, all of this has happened in just a single hour.

Looking back at school, I realize, I will have to come back here tomorrow. I will have to see Chloe, Isabelle, and Zeena. I will have to act as if nothing has happened.

"Let's go to the rock," I say.

I sit with my legs dangling into the crevice. The gritty rock edge bites into the backs of my knees. It feels good, purifying. I imagine jumping. Probably I'm not high enough to actually die, but if I fell right, I could break my neck. Smash my skull.

"That's a really ugly bruise," says Cassandra.

I touch my forehead, feel a lump.

"Did you pass out at any point?"

"No."

"Feel dizzy?"

I try to remember. "The whole thing was a little surreal."

"Yah," says Cassandra heavily.

Then I remember something else. "Where were you?"

"What do you mean?"

"I didn't see you at all today." And, I think, You must have known Chloe was out for blood. If Ella knew it, the whole world did.

"Oh, sweetie . . ." Cassandra frowns, as if she's trying to decide what to tell me. Taking a deep breath, she announces, "Today was a really weird day. It was . . . Ugh, you're going to think I'm such a jerk."

She wants me to deny that.

She sighs. "It's Eamonn's birthday today. Or would have been. So my mom kicked off the day by locking herself in the bedroom and crying hysterically. To which my dad, sensitive being that he is, responded by getting annoyed, because hey, it's been a month, isn't she over losing her child yet? And I was trying to take care of her, and understand him, and think about Eamonn. And by the time I got to school, my whole head was just static. I'm really, really sorry."

I admit, "That's a pretty good excuse."

"I did hear the drama about you and Oliver," she confesses. "I should have known Chloe would react big-time. But I was in one of my bitch modes where it's like, I am dealing with serious, important shit here, leave me alone." She takes my hand. "I will not do that to you again, I promise."

"Thanks." One shred of niceness and I'm a mess again. I have to take a deep, shuddering breath to get past the tears.

Exhaling, I say, "I guess the only good thing is that now it's over."

"What's over?"

"Chloe's whole revenge thing." I gesture to my forehead. "I mean, she pretty much got it."

Cassandra stares down at the playground. The last nannies are dragging the kids home. "You think she thinks that?"

"What more can she do to me?"

"I don't know. What more *can* she do to you?"

I turn my head to see if Cassandra's joking. But she's completely serious.

Get ready for hell.

Cassandra's right. Hell is not a beating in the bathroom. Hell is a place you stay. For all eternity.

Especially now that they know you won't fight back.

I know that's what Cassandra's thinking. And I know what she wants me to do. Use the spells. Fight.

I say, "Three against one is kind of tough."

"Depends on the three," says Cassandra. "Depends on the one. And it's not one, remember?" She points to the air between us. "It's two."

When I don't answer, she sighs, "Or you could just tell the school."

I shake my head. "No way." Telling the school means my parents get involved. It means they hear the whole story with Oliver. My mom gets to hear that I am considered the school slut. My dad gets to think it's all his fault.

"If I go running to the school, maybe Chloe gets suspended.

But she'll just return even more mad and even more determined to get revenge. It won't back her off. It won't . . ."

"Won't what?"

"Make her scared of me."

Cassandra stares at me intently. "Is that what you want?"

I look into the cavern, the rocks and dirt below. I remember the twist of pain as Chloe pulled my hair, how it felt as if my scalp was being ripped off my head. The way she slammed my head against the toilet rim, the stink of the water in my nose. And the laughter. Even when I was choking.

I remember Zeena cracking up. So weak with laughter she had to hold herself up on the sink. Isabelle with her evil smile: *Gotcha!*

I remember the picture on my locker. How I am now everyone's favorite joke.

Cassandra asks, "What do you want?"

As if hypnotized, I have a vision of Chloe, screaming, crying, scrabbling to get away from me. She's wailing *I'm sorry, I'm sorry.* I kick her, feel the sweet satisfaction of viciousness when my foot connects with the target.

"What do you *want*, Antonia?"

"I don't know. I don't know. I don't know." I press the heel of my hand to my aching forehead. "God, I hate myself."

I look up at the sky, as if some great helping hand will descend from the heavens. All I see is gray, indifferent clouds. The buildings that surround the park feel distant and cold. Even the trees are robbed of their color in the sunless late afternoon.

Cassandra takes a deep breath. "You're letting them win."

"I'm not letting them—"

"That's what I did," she interrupts. "With Pretty Boy. Turned all my anger on myself. Hated myself. Hurt myself. Until I figured out how to put the hurt where it belonged."

I want to match Cassandra's energy, but I just can't.

"Okay." She gathers her bag and stands up. "I'm going to let you be."

"You're going?"

"I'm not helping you," she says bluntly. I can't tell if she means she isn't or she won't.

"You're in shock right now," she continues. "You need to be alone. When you figure it out, I'm here."

When I figure it out? I wonder, watching her climb down the rock and leave the park. I can't figure it out. I can't do anything.

But after several minutes, I get up, dust myself off, and head for home. Walking along the edge of the park, I idly let my fingers run over the stone wall. I feel the bump and nubble of the cold rock, the wind blowing off the Hudson River. I am alone. The school won't help me. Ella can't. Even Cassandra, my supposed partner in black magic. She's left me too.

She should have known I was in trouble, I fume. She should have been there for me. We're supposed to be a team.

Entering the lobby of my building, I am strangely relieved to be home. Alone can be good, I think. Maybe it means people leave you be.

In the elevator, I use the safety mirror to arrange my hair so it hides the worst of the bruise. I'll tell my parents I fell in gym class or something.

I hear the voices the second I leave the elevator. First my mom: "For God's sake, Henry." Then my dad: "You have to let this go."

I draw closer to our door. Hear "*I have to let this go? What about her, Henry? Why is she still calling you?*"

"She isn't still calling me, Claire. It was just this once, and it was—"

"How do I know that?"

You don't, I think numbly.

"Tell her it's over," my mom demands.

"I have."

"No. You haven't. Tell her it's over as in you will not speak to her—"

My dad's voice, whining, "Claire, she's not a bad person."

I feel a blast of pure rage. Katherine *is* a bad person. There are bad people in the world who hurt other people and think they have the right. All of a sudden, I remember Chloe walking by me in the hall, her nose in the air over that stupid history project. There was no reason for her to treat me like that. No reason. All her life, people have told her she has the right to treat other people like crap. That she can do whatever she wants.

Well, she can't.

My phone buzzes. I have a text. It's from Cassandra.

It says: *You are not alone.*

I leave my parents' door and go to the stairwell, open the emergency door. Sitting on the concrete steps under the fire hose, I call Cassandra. She picks up right away. I knew she would.

"I know," I tell her. "What I want."

"Okay."

"I want her scared."

"Good."

"I want her scared. I want her hurt. I want her humiliated."

"And?"

My hand shakes a little bit. "I want her gone. Forever."

"Let me think," says Cassandra. "While I think?"

"Yeah?"

"We need something of hers. Something personal, worn next to the skin. Or of the body. Hair. Blood."

"Okay."

"Meet tomorrow after school. My house."

"For?"

"Hex lessons," she says cheerfully, and hangs up.

I tell my parents two things. I fell during gym class and hit my head on the balance beam. I am fine. Everything's fine.

Also—I will be staying over at a friend's house this Saturday.

My parents look at each other. They think they are the reason I want to be out of the house.

They can think that.

CHAPTER NINE

HEX LESSONS. HAIR. SKIN. BLOOD.

"Something wicked this way comes," I whisper to myself as I do my hair the next morning.

I am only slightly kidding.

I check my face in the mirror. My hair covers the bruise just fine. But there is a little swelling by my mouth. I dab on more concealer.

Before I go, I put Aura all alone in the center of the windowsill. The other animals, including Mimi, I move to the shadow sides. Aura is in the sun, taking in its heat and hurting brightness. Aura the serpent.

I meet Ella for the walk to school, praying she doesn't say anything. But she immediately breaks off her hello when she sees the cut on my lip.

She draws closer, gently pushes my hair to one side. Seeing the bruise, she gasps. "Oh, my *God*! I tried calling last night, but there was no answer, and—"

"Please do not freak out." I have to feel strong if I'm going to make it.

She shakes her head. "Toni, for real. This is bad."

"It is what it is," I say. "Can we go now?"

I start walking. Hurrying along beside me, Ella says, "We *have* to tell the school."

"Why? 'Cause I walked into a door?"

"Toni, please, I want to help. I want to do something. Don't shut me out."

For an instant, I feel rotten. But Ella just isn't the kind of friend who can help me with this.

"There's nothing you can do," I say gently. "It's over. Chloe made her point. She'll leave me alone now, I'm pretty sure."

"Well, she better," Ella blazes.

All day, I can feel people checking out my face. They want to ask, but no one does. No one has to, really. Everyone knows what happened: Chloe finally stomped the slut.

I do not see Chloe. Or Zeena. Or Isabelle. I suspect they are avoiding me.

They know what they did to me is serious. They could get in real trouble.

They will. Just not the kind they think.

"We have to weaken her," says Cassandra. We are sitting opposite each other, cross-legged on her rug. We both have cups of her strange, bitter grass tea. The door is shut and locked. The curtains are drawn.

Then she says, "Chloe is strong. Before we strike, we have to work to decrease her power."

"How do we do that?" I ask.

Cassandra smiles. "Increase her fear."

I smile back. "With you so far."

"Chloe may think she's in control now. We have to show her she's not. As I see it, she's vulnerable on two fronts." Cassandra draws a line through the shag of her rug. "One: the school. You could get her expelled for what she did. We have to make her believe that might happen."

Cassandra draws a second line. "Two: Oliver. She's so terrified he wants you back? Good. Let's up the terror quotient."

I shake my head. "If I start flirting with Oliver—"

"What?" Cassandra gazes at me. "She'll beat you up?"

I nod agreement.

"Up till now," says Cassandra, "Chloe's been on the attack. We have to change that. You have to make her feel that she's gone too far. This time, you're coming after her."

"How do we do that?"

I wait for Cassandra's answer. But she doesn't say anything. Instead, she fixes her gaze on me. I meet her eyes, wanting instinctively to show her I am not afraid. Her expression is intense, searching. I glance away for a moment; when I look back, Cassandra is still staring.

"What?" I say finally.

She doesn't answer, just keeps her eyes locked on mine. I swear, I feel heat. Danger.

Panicking, I cry, "What, Cassandra? Just tell me, for God's sake—"

She breaks the gaze. Laughs.

"That," she says, "is a hex."

Before I leave, I ask, "Do we know what we're doing? I mean, what are we aiming for, exactly?"

"Her complete and utter destruction," says Cassandra.

I totally cannot tell: is she joking or not?

Then she laughs. "No, seriously. When you say 'gone forever,' I get it that you mean metaphorically, not actually . . . dead."

I pretend to think. "Hm, not so sure . . ."

"How about powerless?" offers Cassandra, as if she's a waitress. *Would madame prefer the chocolate mousse or the cheesecake today?*

"Maybe a little humiliated?" I suggest jokingly. *Madame will have Tête de Chloe on a blood-soaked platter, please.*

Then I remember the Threefold Law. That whatever you send out comes back to you at three times the power. Maybe I need to rethink.

Only, what Cassandra said about Oliver, how he silenced me so it was just payback when I silenced him, counts here too. Chloe attacked me and left me feeling dead inside. I remember sitting on this same rock, how lifeless and empty I felt. Like I was absolutely nothing.

That's what I want for Chloe.

When I get home, I practice hexes in the mirror. Trying to see only my eyes, I draw closer and closer to my reflection. My eyes begin to ache; I feel dizzy. When I am close, they start to merge, form a single circle of sight, like the barrel of a gun.

The evil eye.

* * *

The next day, I am catching a drink at the water fountain when I see them. Chloe and Zeena and Isabelle.

Isabelle actually gasps. Right away, she turns and finds something on a nearby bulletin board to stare at.

Chloe is frozen. So am I. My heart is pounding. My feet are numb. I want more than anything to run away, to not be near them.

But that's exactly what I must not do.

My hand grips the water fountain.

I fix my eyes on Chloe. Only Chloe. She's the power center, but she takes strength from the other two. If I can isolate her, she will be weakened.

I see surprise in her eyes as they meet mine. She opens her mouth, then closes it.

The water is still running. I will not take my thumb off the button. I imagine it's Chloe's heart I'm pressing, pressing until it bursts.

You know what you did, I say in my mind. You know. And know this: payback is coming.

Zeena lifts her elbow to nudge Chloe. Chloe angrily shoves it away.

"Come on, guys," she says, and stumbles through the hallway door.

Use others. That's another thing Cassandra told me. Everyone likes to talk about me? Fine. Let them talk. Only this time, I'm giving them the story.

So when Nina Watts sidles up to me after chemistry and says, "Any updates on the Oliver sitch?" I look from side to side, supposedly to make sure no one but Nina is listening. Knowing the universal sign for good dirt, Nina leans in.

"I don't know," I sigh. "It's so messed up."

Her eyes widen. "How so?"

I do another look-around as we settle by the hallway windows. "Well, you know Chloe's a little . . . angry with me?"

Nina frowns. "Uh-huh."

"And I'm like, over it. Oliver—she can have him." Nina looks disappointed; she is hoping for a torrid triangle. Instead, I give her, "Here's the thing."

She perks up.

I lean in, whisper, "He won't leave me alone."

"Oh, my God," she hisses.

"I know. And I'm like, Dude, seriously, it's over."

"And he says what?"

"He misses me. He wants us to be—" I roll my eyes: *Who knows.* I am, I tell myself, merely quoting what Oliver actually said. If it lands him in a pile of doo-doo, so be it. Welcome to my world, Oliver.

"And you're . . . not into it?" Nina wants to get the story straight before she passes it on to everyone at school.

"No," I say firmly. "It was one thing when he and Chloe were split up and he felt sad—"

"I thought she was in Europe."

"Yeah, that's her version," I say sarcastically. "But they're together now and I have zero interest. I wish he would get that."

Nina raises an eyebrow. "He probably wants out with the she-devil. I mean, who could blame him? She's one harsh lady when she wants to be."

Then she leans back in. "Hey—between you and me—did she go crazy on you in a bathroom?"

I have thought and thought about how to play this. I say slowly, "Between you and me? Yes."

I pull back my hair to show the bruise. Nina says, "Holy—"

"I think Chloe's losing it," I say. "Part of me is actually worried about her."

"Worried? Screw her. Are you going to tell the school? You should. It's insane."

"I don't know. I haven't decided yet."

Then I touch her arm. "Do me a favor? Don't spread this around."

"Oh, I won't," says Nina earnestly. "Although people should know how crazy she is." She points to my forehead. "That's so not right."

Finally, I think. People are seeing it my way.

I know what time Chloe leaves for lunch. I know because I used to make every effort to avoid the lobby when she was headed in or out. On Wednesday, at precisely 1:10, I make sure to be there.

Right outside the office of Ms. Petrie, the guidance counselor.

I wait until Chloe comes out of the stairwell, wait until she's actually seen me. Then I call out, "Thanks, Ms. Petrie, I will." Then I walk slowly toward Chloe. I keep my eye on her every step of the way. Chloe knows that if I'm going to rat her out, Ms. Petrie is the person to talk to.

I can see from her expression that she's trying to come up with something cutting. "Snitch," "Whiner," something like that.

Only she's too scared. In her entire life, Chloe has never been called out for her crap. Never once been held responsible. And now she thinks she might be.

"Everyone knows," I murmur as I pass by.

The next day, Wallace reports that Imelda the cafeteria lady accidentally splashed some tomato sauce on Chloe's sleeve as she was passing a plate of ravioli to Zeena. Chloe went ballistic, shrieking at Imelda and threatening to get her fired.

This is serious. It's one thing for Chloe to abuse all of us; it's another for her to pick on people who work in the cafeteria. A, it's supremely uncool. And B, they won't put up with it.

Wallace says, "Good thing Isabelle pulled her out of there; those ladies were ready to take a ladle to Chloe's nonexistent behind."

"Chloe seems very stressed out these days," I say serenely.

That afternoon, Ella says, "Okay, I know you don't care about Oliver—"

"Correct."

"But Rachel Davenport told me that Eric Koslowski told her that Oliver found out what Chloe did to you and he's, like, totally freaked."

Oliver freaked, I think. What else is new?

Then Ella adds, "So maybe he'll do something."

"Ella, if Oliver were a knight, he'd only show up when the princess was toast and the dragon was picking her out of his teeth."

As I say it, I realize that's the kind of joke Cassandra might make.

Ella hears it too. After a moment, she says, "How's Cass?"

I try to look startled. "I don't know."

"No, I just thought . . . maybe you guys were getting to be friends."

I do not want to outright lie to Ella. "Maybe friend*ly*."

She nods hurriedly. Then blurts out, "Just . . ."

"What?"

Her hands jump into the air. "No, I get it. You guys are totally cool, you should be friends? Only . . ."

Don't forget about me.

I touch my head to hers. "You're still my everything, babes."

Cassandra's parents are going to visit friends for the weekend. "Because sitting in someone else's house not talking about Eamonn is going to be so much better than sitting here and not talking about him," says Cassandra that afternoon as we make final plans in the park.

"Do they mind you're not going?" I ask, thinking my parents would never let me spend the weekend on my own.

Cassandra says, "Are you kidding? They're relieved. So come over Saturday and we'll do it. Do you have the item yet?"

"Not yet."

"Get it, Antonia. We're running out of time. How's the hexing going?"

I nod. "I think she's on the run."

"That's where we want her. Just get the item and we're set."

The item. Something of or worn close to the body. On Friday in English, I consider my options. I could steal a piece of Chloe's clothing. I could steal her water bottle and hope for backwash. Collect nail clippings. Hand her a towel to wipe her sweat off. It won't be easy.

Later that morning I'm on my way to art class when I hear shouts coming from the gym. Drawn by the metallic clang of a ball on wood, the squeak of sneakers, and cries of "I got it, I got it," I peer through the glass window.

Basketball. There's Chloe, laughing as she misses a pass.

How can she laugh? I wonder. How can she feel happy and careless when she's wrecked my life?

I crack the gym door, look inside. In the corner, a heap of backpacks. I spot Chloe's Marc Jacobs bag right away. She's placed it carefully on top so it doesn't get squashed by the other, lesser bags.

Mr. Finley, the gym teacher, is a fanatic about stretching. Everyone stretches before a game, everyone stretches after. And it's all very orderly. You line up in two rows with your backs to the door. All eyes on Mr. Finley. Who in turn watches closely.

While everyone's bent over, stretching their hamstrings, I creep in the door, snatch Chloe's bag. It takes two seconds to find her hairbrush. I grip the bristles in my fist, pull. Get a lovely, thick tangle of hair.

Then I put the brush back in the bag, toss the bag back on the heap.

Chloe's flip-out in the cafeteria does not go unnoticed. As Ella tells me at lunch, "They were going to suspend her. For real. But her parents said she was having this really hard time, so the principal let her get away with writing Imelda an apology."

"Having a hard time?" I'm trying to play uninterested about Chloe, but this gets me. "That spoiled brat—give me a break. She's got people so snowed."

"I don't know," Ella says uncertainly. "I saw her in the bathroom yesterday and she was popping a pill. Like, a prescription."

"'Mommy, Daddy, I'm so upset, let me take some lovely downers. . . .'"

Ella looks at me anxiously. "Plus I heard Oliver's dumping her. And that he's already crushing on someone else?"

I can feel Ella's curiosity. *Is that someone you?*

I say, "It's called karma. Those who fling poo shall get it back— right in the kisser."

That afternoon, I leave school with Chloe's hair in a sealed pouch. Everything will be different when I come back on Monday, I think. Better.

That's when I see them on the corner. Oliver and Chloe.

Oliver's shoulders are hunched, his head down, one hand gripping his backpack. A turtle, I think, shrinking into his shell. Chloe is standing in front of him. I can't hear what she's saying. But from the way she's throwing her arms around and jerking her head, I would guess it's nothing nice.

I start walking toward them. Partly out of curiosity, partly because . . . I can.

As I get closer, I hear Chloe say, "Just *talk* to me, Oliver. Say something."

I wait, along with Chloe. Oliver shakes his head.

Chloe reaches for his arm. Her voice breaking a little, she says, "You're freezing me out and I can't take it."

Unfortunately, that happens to be when I pass them. Caught in her moment of weakness, Chloe spins toward me. Oliver murmurs, "No, Chloe, don't—"

She shrieks. "Can't you ever leave us alone? What do I have to do to get you away from us?"

It hurts for an instant, Chloe's vision of me as some needy, pathetic loser who's always crawling for her scraps. But then I remember Cassandra. I remember the plan.

"Maybe you're the one who has to go away, Chloe," I say. "You ever think of that?"

CHAPTER TEN

SATURDAY AFTERNOON, I TAKE **MIMI** and put her in the corner of the windowsill in a slice of cool, dark shade. Then I take Dallas, Boo Boo, Phoebe, and Gloriana and put them in a little circle with their backs to her.

I take Aura, put her next to Mimi. Mimi needs her power. She can't do this alone.

Cassandra told me to come at ten o'clock. It feels creepy walking to her house this late. I keep looking over my shoulder, worried someone's following me.

Walter is on the door and he touches the brim of his hat when I approach. "Ms. Cassandra?" he asks. I nod. "I'll buzz and let her know. You can go ahead."

I walk into the hall-of-mirrors lobby. An old lady comes out her door with a dachshund. I hear his little nails *click, click, click* on the floor. The lady saying, "Come on, Chowsie." Walter saying, "Evening, Ms. Abernathy." "Good evening, Walter."

The elevator door slides open. I step in and ride up.

When I ring the bell, Cassandra throws open the door, says, "Abandon pity all ye who enter!"

I laugh. Drop my bag on the floor. "Nice to be here."

"Ain't a parent-free house a little slice of heaven on rye?"

Cassandra is wearing a black turtleneck and black jeans. Her hair is back, so her cheekbones are super sharp. She looks great.

I look down at my skirt and red tights; the only black thing I'm wearing is my hair bow. "Was I supposed to do all black?"

"Nah—no biggie. Just felt like going with the obvious. Some wine?" She points out a bottle on the dining room table.

"*Mais oui*," I say, although I don't usually drink except at parties. Cassandra pours me an enormous glass. "Whoa."

"My parents'll never miss it," she says, pouring herself one. "My dad's been drinking so much, he'll just think he went overboard one night."

She gestures to her room. "Bring your glass. And the bag."

As we go through Cassandra's door, I say, "Okay!" She's really done it up. A dozen fat red candles are burning. A spicy incense makes the place smoky and mysterious. She's draped the window with a black cloth. In the center of the room, she's placed an old battered pot. It's black with colored spatters. Around it is a circle of charms of some kind. Shells and stones, and twisted little figures I can't quite make out. Two scrolls tied with black ribbon lean against the pot.

There is also a knife. Slim, with a black-and-gold striped handle. It looks very sharp. For a moment, I wonder if that's what Cassandra used on her wrists. Then I wonder how we're using it tonight.

"*Salut!*" she says, clinking my glass. As we drink, I immediately notice this wine is a lot less sweet and syrupy than the party plonk I'm used to. Maybe it's the incense—or the fact that I was too psyched to eat much today—but two sips go straight to my head.

For a little while we talk about school stuff. Cassandra's dumped rugby. Rolling her eyes, she says, "Lizbeth was like, 'Come back when you're ready.' I was like, 'Yeah, never going to be ready.'"

Then she sits up, asks, "So you got it?"

I have Chloe's hair safely stored in a plastic bag. Now I take it out, hold it up.

"Let's put it in the stewpot," says Cassandra cheerfully. I drop it in. It's so light and brittle. That's how I want Chloe to feel: a dry, fragile bit of nothing.

"Okay," says Cassandra, rearranging herself slightly so we are sitting at either end of the pot. "'Tis the midnight hour."

She takes a swig of wine, waits until I do the same. Then she hands me one of the scrolls—heavy, yellowed paper. I tug the black ribbon loose, unroll it. Cassandra has written the words of the spell in thick black ink. There's a violence to the writing; the letters look scratched into the surface of the paper.

I'm about to say "A for penmanship," but I hear in my head, *No more jokes.*

I take a sip of wine.

"Go easy," says Cassandra, gently directing my wrist to set the glass down.

She picks up the knife, then, with one quick, savage cut, slices the ball of her thumb open. Blood wells up, starts to drip.

"Now you," she says, thrusting the knife at me. "Come on, hurry."

Panicked at what I have to do—I can never match Cassandra's

guts—I fumble with the knife. It falls on the floor. Blood smears the rug.

"Crap, I'm sorry—"

"Forget it. Do it."

I grab the knife, press it against my hand. Bracing myself for the pain, I push. But I'm not ruthless enough; the skin stays whole. No blood comes.

Blood is dripping down Cassandra's wrist.

"Here," she says, and takes hold of my wrist. Before I know it, she's sliced me open. It stings—more than stings, burns—but then she's pressing the palm of her hand against mine, holding them over the pot. Slowly, the blood starts to drip on the hair. Fascinated, I watch as it falls, heavy and thick onto the dry strands, flattening them, collapsing them. Overpowering them.

"The first five lines," whispers Cassandra. "Say them now."

My voice shaking, I read,

> *"My curse shall haunt you, and my hate*
> *No victim's blood shall expiate.*
> *With crooked nails your cheeks I'll tear*
> *And, squatting on your bosoms, scare*
> *With hideous fears your sleep away!"*

Finished, I look up at Cassandra. Her eyes are bright, fierce. Letting go of my hand, she picks up one of the candles.

"Give me your ribbon," she says softly.

It takes me a moment to realize she means my hair tie. I reach back, pull the bow off. I hand it to her. She holds the bow over the candle's flame, lights it on fire. Then she drops it into the pot. Instantly, the hair flames up, threatens to leap out of the pot, engulf the room.

"Quick," she says. "The rest of the spell."

My voice is stronger this time, my delivery better now that I'm used to the rhythm.

> *"Then shall mob, some future day,*
> *Pelt you from street to street with stones,*
> *Till, falling dead, ye filthy crones,*
> *The dogs and wolves and carrion fowl*
> *That make the Esquiline their prowl*
> *In banquet horrible and grim*
> *Shall tear your bodies limb from limb."*

The fire is dead. All that's left is smoke that stings my eyes and makes me cough. Raising her wineglass into the smoke, Cassandra closes her eyes and says, "Hecate, we call upon you to deliver your servant Antonia from the malice of Chloe Nachmias. Use your power, Hecate. Render Chloe Nachmias helpless. Sap her spirit, cut off her energy. Let your servant know the sweet thrill of vengeance on those who have wronged her."

Drink.

I do, draining the last of the wine.

"Okay," says Cassandra. "Done."

For no reason, I burst out laughing. Then I'm crying. It's so intense. What did we just do? Cassandra gathers me up, hugs me. Her arms feel good and strong and safe. Stroking my hair, she says, "It's okay, baby, it's okay. We did it. You're safe now, she can't hurt you."

Waving a hand in front of her face, Cassandra gets up to open a window. "Witchcraft is stinky, hey?"

Laughing weakly, I say, "Sorry I screwed up the cutting."

"Don't worry. I was prepared. Doesn't matter who does the cutting, blood's blood. You did very well."

She hoists the window up. A blast of fresh air blows into the room. I breathe deep. Normal is still out there. We haven't destroyed it, I think crazily.

Cassandra points to my hand, waves her own. "We should clean up."

Cassandra is so prepared she even has gauze pads and hydrogen peroxide ready in the bathroom. As she dabs disinfectant on my hand, I see it's really not that deep a cut.

"Maybe a little scar," says Cassandra.

This makes me think of her scars. "What were you feeling?" I ask. "When you—" I nod to her wrists.

Cassandra wrinkles her nose. "An early attempt at a spell—the pity spell. The 'Oh, I'll hurt myself and he'll come running' spell. The kind that never, ever works." She raises an eyebrow at me, lays the gauze over my cut.

"God, I'd have come running."

She smiles. "Yes, but we know this about you. You still have pity in your heart." She draws a light X just above my breast. "One day, it shall be gone."

"Not totally, I hope." I smooth out the tape at the edge of the gauze. "I mean, kind of sucky world otherwise."

"It is a kind of sucky world," she says. "Come on. Bedtime."

We have one more glass of wine, then pour the rest down the drain. "Remind me," says Cassandra, "to take the evidence to recycling tomorrow."

We clear away the pot and the candles. Each candle gets blown out, placed on the windowsill. The pot is washed, dried, put back in the kitchen. "My mom's next batch of chili will be interesting," says Cassandra. I giggle.

I want to ask Cassandra just what kind of spell we cast. What kind of thing might happen to Chloe?

Then I feel—or know this is what Cassandra would tell me—it's done. Whatever will happen will happen. No point in worrying now.

I don't think I've ever felt so exhausted. I practically fall onto the old futon Cassandra lays on the floor next to her bed. My body sinks into the padding; I've never been so grateful to rest.

Cassandra switches off the light. I hear the slither of cloth as she gets under the covers. For a few minutes—or maybe hours, who knows, I'm so out of it—no one says anything.

Then Cassandra asks, "What's the worst thing that's ever happened to you?"

I come back to consciousness. "Me?" Knowing what Cassandra's answer to that question would be, I feel oddly unworthy; what do I have that compares?

Then I think of Katherine's snarky, choking *"Basketball."* But I've never told anyone, not even Ella, about that. Telling would make it real.

But it is real. Maybe we don't talk about it, maybe Katherine's not around anymore, but she's like a ghost haunting the house. And I know now: Spirits have power. They do real harm.

In the dark, I prepare myself to say the words out loud: My dad had an affair.

First I say, "This is a don't-tell-anyone, okay?"

"Obviously."

"This summer, we found out my dad was having an affair. With someone practically my age."

Cassandra breathes, "Oh, shit."

I don't want Cassandra thinking my dad is some kind of psycho perv, so I say, "I mean, she was a grad student, but—"

"Still."

"Yeah."

"So that's what happened this summer," she says slowly, putting it together. "Did you know her?"

"Yeah, she was around the house all the time. My mom really liked her. They were almost friends, you know?" As I say this, I remember how great it was whenever Katherine was around. She was this exciting, energetic person from the real world bursting in on our dusty little cave.

"Wow," says Cassandra. "So your mom had no idea."

"No."

"Did you?"

I'm about to say no, of course not. But then I remember being in the kitchen with Katherine and my dad. We were eating Italian macaroons from this bakery in Brooklyn where Katherine lived. And I thought, This is so cool, the three of us. So much better than . . .

Cassandra says, "Some people are good at that, getting people to like them."

"Well, I don't like her anymore," I say.

"Oh, they always end up betraying you," says Cassandra. "It's just about getting you to like them. When you need them to do something for you—"

"Like stop sleeping with your dad."

"Yeah, kinda. They're ego monsters."

"Totally."

I tell her about Katherine coming to the house, how she blurted out the news, then acted like I was the one hurting her.

"Then she went and called my dad and told *him*. And I'm sure she thinks she was being noble—"

"But really, she wanted to force it so he would leave your mom."

"Exactly! I totally think that."

"Evil," says Cassandra simply. "But your dad ditched her instead?"

"Yeah."

"Glad she got what she deserved."

I hesitate. Did she? If so, why don't we all feel better?

I shake my head, clearing it. Without thinking, I say, "What about you? What's the worst—"

Then I remember. In my head: *Oh, my God, I'm so sorry*—

"Don't be sorry," says Cassandra casually. "I know I didn't want to go into it before. But I don't want a big sign over my head—

Warning: Do Not Speak of the Bad Thing. It happened. Not talking about it doesn't change that."

"No, but—"

"The weirdest thing was he was quiet," she says, as if I haven't spoken. "When I went in, the water was like a blanket. Here, sweetie, let's tuck you in. His eyes were closed. His hair waving under the surface. He looked calm and peaceful. I actually thought, Oh, sweet."

I see it completely clearly, as if I am standing in the doorway of the bathroom, staring down at Eamonn. There is nothing I can say. I hope Cassandra can feel how my heart hurts for her.

"Insane, right?"

"No. You didn't know."

"Oh, I knew," she says matter-of-factly. "The second I didn't hear him. If Eamonn was quiet, he had to be dead. But it wasn't awful for him. That's what I worried about at first. That it had been this terrible thing while he was drowning and he was scared and alone when he died. But when I really looked at him, I knew it was okay."

"He probably didn't have any idea, right?"

"No. They think he had a seizure, hit his head, and passed out. So no fear and not a lot of pain. It's not a terrible way to go."

Cassandra is trying to sound practical. But in the darkness, I feel a wild fluttering, frantic wings of terror, and . . .

Grief?

Anger?

There's another feeling there. The beat is more erratic, panicky. She's trying hard to keep it quiet; I feel her effort to stay calm, hide her thoughts.

Guilt?

I hear her say, "No one will say it? Like, my mom and dad? But they're relieved. On some level. We all knew Eamonn was going to be a bigger problem the older he got. Poor kid. Can you imagine? Everyone seeing you as this . . . burden? A drag? No wonder he never stopped screaming."

She pauses. "But I was good at knowing what he needed. Everyone kind of counted on me for that. So I feel like it was okay. In a way, I gave him what he needed."

Puzzled, I say, "What?"

There's a silence. Then Cassandra yawns. "What can I say? My parents just left us alone one too many times. Anyway, do you mind if we don't talk about this anymore?" she asks.

"Yeah, of course."

I wait for her to bring up something else, start another game. As the silence stretches, I realize that's all for tonight. Cassandra's not asleep. I can feel her energy awake and watchful in the dark. But she's gone into hiding.

My parents just left us alone one too many times. What does that mean? Ella said something about this, something that I need to put together with what Cassandra said. Because I don't quite understand—

Then I feel bad, snooping through Cassandra's life for some ugly secret. There is no secret. Of course she feels guilty. I would too, if my little brother died and I was supposed to be watching him. There's no way you don't feel it was your fault.

I wonder how her parents are, if they blame her in some way. That would be truly horrible.

Go to sleep.

Go to sleep.

Cassandra's voice sings in my head, gentle and soft. Friendly. As if she knows what I've been thinking and doesn't mind. But she does want me to quit now.

Close your sweet brown eyes.

I smile. Close my eyes. After a few moments, I start to drift.

She sang that song to Eamonn.

The thought comes out of nowhere, jolting me awake. My first frightened notion is that Cassandra has heard me. I feel for anger, hurt . . .

Hear Cassandra snoring.

Settling back, I think, And so what if she sang that song to Eamonn? He was her baby brother. It doesn't mean anything dire.

I'm so, so tired.

But it takes me a while to fall asleep.

CHAPTER ELEVEN

THE NEXT MORNING, I OPEN my eyes to the sound of Cassandra humming in the distance. I am alone, she's somewhere else in the apartment. I don't recognize the tune, but it's happy, silly—a making-breakfast tune.

There's sunlight peeking through the curtains; I've never been here in daylight. It's not a cave or a witches' den. Just an ordinary, messy room.

My head hurts. My stomach feels like it has a heavy, greasy ball rolling around in it. Every once in a while, I think I might throw up.

Cassandra appears at the door. "Coffee? Cheerios? English muffin?"

"Coffee," I croak. "Definitely."

Coffee, as always, is the answer. Sitting at the breakfast table, I manage half an English muffin. Cassandra is wolfing down Cheerios; the bowl's hardly emptied and she's pouring more from the box. They make a happy little rattle as they clatter into the bowl, which has a bright daisy on the side.

"You seem . . . really good," I say blearily.

"I *am* really good," she says. "Way good, stupendous, and great. Casting a really intense spell is like . . . sorry . . . a spiritual laxative. Just takes all the crap inside you and sends it on its merry way."

Heading right toward Chloe, I think. I sip my coffee. "When do you think it'll hit?"

Cassandra pretends to look at her watch. "Um, at ten-forty-seven Eastern Standard Time." She rolls her eyes. "Who knows?"

"But . . ."

Cassandra smiles. "Look, there probably won't be any big boom. We've blocked her energy."

Blocked? Is that it? Some of the things we said were pretty extreme. I try to remember the words, what we actually asked for. But it's all a wine-queasy blur.

"She can't hurt you anymore, that's all that matters. Monday, when we're back at school—you'll see. I bet she's scared to come near you."

The thought of Chloe scared cheers me up. "Pass the butter," I say. "And maybe some jam."

It hits as I am walking home. I am walking from Columbus to Amsterdam when the moment comes. The autumn chill in the air eases. The day becomes fresh, rather than fierce and biting. My shoulders feel looser, like when you shrug off a heinously heavy backpack. I take a huge gulp of air, realize my chest doesn't feel so tight. The last few weeks tumble out of reality and into the past.

It's over, I think. I'm free. Chloe no longer has power over me.

I can do anything, go anywhere I want.

The world is mine again.

I bounce into the house and hand my mom a sunflower. I bought it on the way home. I was so happy, I wanted to give someone something.

Taking it, my mom smiles and says, "My, my—thank you."

I flop down at the dining room table. From the kitchen, my mom asks, "How was the sleepover? Did you get any sleep?"

As I try to answer her question, the memory of last night hits, and with it, a feeling of . . . ugliness. Shame. Now that I'm home, talking to my mom, I don't want to think about burning things and cutting myself. It's like taking something you thought was beautiful in the store and holding it up to the light once you get home to find it's all cheap and cracked. You feel stupid for buying it.

"Fine," I say, tugging my sleeve over my hand. "What'd you guys do?"

"Oh . . . ," says my mom vaguely. As she puts a small vase with the flower in it at the center of the table, she catches me fiddling with my sleeve and says sharply, "What happened to your hand?"

"Gym dumbness," I say, wishing I'd been smart enough to take the bandage off.

She's about to say more when my phone rings, sharp and loud in the Sunday quiet. "Ah—teen crisis," says my mom. "I'll leave you to it."

I dig in my bag for the phone. For a brief, silly moment, I

wonder if it's Chloe. Then feel happy when I realize I don't care if it is or not. I'm beyond that.

But it's not Chloe. It's Ella.

"Hey, Ella," I say, happy to hear from her.

"Hey." She sounds out of breath, as usual.

Then she says, "So, I don't know if you heard."

Instantly, my entire body goes on alert. "No."

"Um—oh, God, this is awful. I mean, really bad."

"What, Ella? Just tell me!"

My mom draws close, a worried look on her face.

"It's Chloe—"

My stomach wrenches. I am going to throw up, here and now, on my parents' hall rug.

"What?" I demand.

"I know you didn't like her, I know she was horrible to you—"

Walls, ice-cold iron walls, slam down on all four sides of me. There is no room. No air. I am trapped. *I know you didn't like her.* It's an accusation, a pointed finger. The world knows I hated Chloe.

And while I am struggling for air, Ella is saying things like last night and party and coming home and truck. And it all jumbles in my head and it kind of makes sense but I still don't know what's going on.

". . . and this morning, she died. At the hospital. She—"

And Ella can't say any more. She just starts crying.

What time? I want to ask her. What time did she die?

But I can't. I don't have to. I know what time Chloe died. I know exactly when. I know where I was, what I was doing.

I was walking from Columbus to Amsterdam. Feeling free.

* * *

What happened is this.

Chloe was at Alison Maxwell's birthday party. It was a twenties theme. To Alison's parents, this meant flappers, jazz, copies of F. Scott Fitzgerald on the tables. To Alison and some of her friends, it meant sneaking in alcohol like they would have done during Prohibition. Which they would have done no matter what the theme was, but it gave them a fun excuse to hide mini bottles in their bags. Once Alison's parents went out for the evening, they tumbled the booze out on the floor and everyone grabbed some, like kids at a piñata party.

Chloe had a lot of mini bottles, apparently. She may have had some other things too. She spent much of the night huddled in a corner with Isabelle. Most people avoided her; she was in a ranty mood and being a "downer."

At around one in the morning, the party broke up. Chloe headed home. Both she and Alison live on Fifth Avenue in the Seventies, so she decided to walk. People were a little worried because she was pretty out of it. But they let her go, thinking, Hey, it's only a few blocks.

To get home, Chloe had to cross three streets. At Seventy-Second Street, she didn't see that the light was red. She didn't see the truck come barreling around the corner. She just wandered out into the middle of the street.

They got her to the hospital. So her parents were with her. When she died.

It's been ten minutes since I hung up with Ella. I can't get up off the floor. My mom keeps asking if there's something she can do.

My dad keeps asking questions. Things like "Did you know her well?" "Did she usually drink a lot?" "Did she have a fight with someone?" "How much do kids drink at these parties?" "Are they charging the driver?"

"Henry," says my mom. "Stop."

"What?"

"Stop looking for a rational reason this girl died. It's just a"— she gropes for the word—"a tragedy. A senseless, awful tragedy. It's nothing she did."

She strokes my hair, says softly, "It's nothing anybody did."

One o'clock, I think for the nine thousandth time. Midnight to one. Last night was so crazy, I don't remember time in a normal way.

That's what I tell myself. But way back in the corner of my brain, a tiny echo of Cassandra's voice saying, "'Tis the midnight hour."

It means nothing, I think fiercely. You're stupid, you're insane. Stop this fantasy that because you got drunk and burned some hair you have some sacred magic power that pushes cars into people.

But Chloe was not a big drinker. She didn't get stupid, never threw up. How could she not see a truck coming? How could she not hear it? You hear those things rumbling blocks away.

I want to talk to Cassandra so badly. Because there's other stuff I don't remember. The spell was to block her energy—not destroy it. Not . . . wipe it out. Right? We just wanted to stop her hurting me.

I send these thoughts out to the air. Hear back, *Bullshit.* My voice in my head or Cassandra's?

Okay, even if it is bullshit. Even if I did want to hurt Chloe, I never said "death," did I? There was nothing in that spell . . .

144

Then shall mob, some future day,
Pelt you from street to street with stones,
Till, falling dead . . .

A street. No stones. Just a truck. A two-ton truck hurtling at a hundred-pound girl, throwing her in the air till she lands ten feet away, her body broken. . . .

Shall tear your bodies limb from limb.

Oh, God, I did not mean this. I did not mean for this to happen.

I stand up suddenly. "I have to be alone right now," I say, and go to my room.

The second the door's closed, I call Cassandra. I have trouble punching in the numbers; three tries to get it right. My fingers are not working at all. I'm a jangle of disconnected wires.

As the phone rings, I think, She has to answer. She has to. She's the only one who can tell me what that spell could do. The only one who can say, "Chill. I just did it to make you feel stronger. It was a head game. There is no power to this stuff at all."

It rings for a long time. Then goes to voice mail.

I hang up. Dial again. Again no answer.

My heart is banging in my chest. I don't so much put the phone down as let it fall out of my hand.

Cassandra won't talk to me. That means every awful thing I'm trying not to think is true. It means Cassandra knows what happened to Chloe and doesn't want any contact between us.

Because we're guilty. We sent something out into the world, and it killed Chloe.

145

I slide down the wall, pull myself in tight. I feel terrified of moving, aware that even the slightest motion could set off something that I never intended. I am hyperaware of my body, the ripples in the air caused by my breathing. The way my heat changes the atmosphere. If I move even a finger, it could change something. If I even think the wrong thing . . .

I see the truck, Chloe turning.

They say it sounds like a bomb going off, when a truck hits someone at high speed.

A little while later, there's a knock at the door. My mother's voice: "Honey?"

"No," I say.

The door opens anyway. "Oh, baby—"

My mom makes me take a shower. "I promise," she says firmly. "It helps."

And it does help. The blast of the water drowns out the panic, leaves me stripped of emotion.

Chloe died because she was hit by a truck, I think tiredly as I wrap myself in a towel. You were not driving the truck. You did not kill her. You got no sleep last night and you are really not in your right mind.

"Take a nap," says my mom when I come out of the bathroom.

"Mom, it's lunchtime." My voice is all croaky and raw.

My phone rings. I hesitate, because it's probably someone wanting to do the grief freak about Chloe, and for a million reasons, I'm not up for that.

I look at the name. It's Cassandra. I wave my mom away.

"How are you?" she says, her voice strong and cheerful. "Feel like a walk in the park?"

We meet by the reservoir in Central Park. It's a gray, chilly afternoon. Diehards are jogging around and around the huge pool of water, which is surrounded by a chain-link fence—I guess so people don't fall in.

Cassandra stands directly on the path, slurping a smoothie from Fruitopia. When joggers glare as they make their detour past her, she smiles around the straw.

But when she sees me, she comes over and gives me a one-armed hug. "Hey," she says.

Tearing up, I put my head on her shoulder. "Oh, my God, Cassandra. Oh, my God."

"Come on now," she croons. "Keep it together."

"What did we do?"

I look at her, because I really need her to answer that question.

She takes a slurp of her smoothie. "No one's going to arrest us for chanting some half-assed poem."

I stop, move away from her. "Half-assed poem or not, Cassandra, Chloe is dead. Okay? Seriously—"

"'She's really most sincerely dead,'" sings Cassandra in a Munchkin voice. "'Tra, la, la, la.'"

"Cassandra!" I shout, trying to jolt her into understanding what's happened here.

But then I think, Maybe Cassandra knows exactly what's happened here.

She smiles.

"This is not what I asked for," I insist. "I never wanted Chloe—"

Cassandra narrows her eyes. "Really? Because I seem to remember the D word coming up."

"From *you*."

"So, what exactly does 'gone forever' mean?"

Struggling to stay calm, I say, "You said you understood it was a metaphor."

I search her eyes, looking for some sign of my friend. I can't tell: Is she totally messing with me? Is this her way of dealing with what's happened? I think, Cassandra, please tell me we did not use a killing spell. Just say the freaking words.

But she just nods. "Ah." And starts walking again.

Running behind, I say, "Tell me that's not what we asked for."

She shrugs. "You never know how these things are going to play out. We wanted her energy stopped."

"We said blocked."

She rolls her eyes.

"There's a *difference*."

Cassandra puts her hands in her pockets. "Maybe that was the only way to keep her from harming you. Maybe her will was that strong."

I feel like I'm falling. As if I've backed away from the cliff's edge, only to tumble off the other side. "No," I whisper. "No."

Cassandra whirls around. "*Why* are you so hung up on this? How can you, of all people, feel guilty? Do you have total amnesia about what this chick did to you?"

My head hitting the rim of the toilet, the feeling that I was going to puke it hurt so bad. Shit floating in the water, past my face. Yes, I think, she deserved it, she deserved all of it.

"Okay?" Cassandra puts a hand on my arm. "Really, this is not someone to weep over."

Everyone's someone to weep over, I think, at least to someone.

"This is not happening," I whisper. "It just can't be."

"I get why you're anxious," says Cassandra in a "Now, let's be practical" voice. "Power is scary. In some ways, it's easier to be the victim."

I'm so tired it's hard to put words together. But I manage to say, "There's an in-between, isn't there? The normal person who doesn't hurt other people, just does her own thing?" Like, do we all have to be predators and prey? Are those the only choices?

"There are a lot of people who like to think that's what they are. Personally, I think it's better to know you have the power to hurt people—and use it well." She hugs me, then looks deep into my eyes. "Which we *did*."

Cassandra's certainty is the only thing I have to hold on to right now. I close my eyes, try to stop thinking about it.

I hear Cassandra say, "Okay. Tomorrow?"

Oh, God—school. Everyone freaking out. Oliver. I say, "I'm calling in sick."

"No, that's what we don't do. You have to go. And everyone's going to be all Boo-hoo, Chloe was such a great girl. And you're going to feel like crap. But when that happens? Remember what she did to you. Remember who she really was. And know you did the right thing."

She walks away. Alone on the path, I watch her. And think, What *did* we do, Cassandra? What did you make me do?

And the answer comes.

Nothing you didn't want.

* * *

That night, I check out people's Facebook postings on Chloe. *I can't believe this! Her poor family! Rest in peace, sweet Chloe! You were the best, the most beautiful!* At first, it hits me like a kick in the gut: all this hysterical love for my total enemy.

But then the pain twists into anger. What are these idiots talking about? Sweet? Best? Give me a break. We need a serious reality check here.

I put my fingers on the keyboard, think, Yeah, rest in peace, Chloe. Lord knows you were such an angry, spiteful bitch, you never gave anybody peace when you were alive.

My fingers are hovering over the keys, ready to type, when there's a knock on the door. I jump, squeak, "Yeah?"

My dad puts his head in. "Hi there."

Flustered, I say, "Oh, sorry, is it dinner or—"

"Nope," he says calmly, coming in and closing the door. "Just wanted to see how you are."

I grope for an acceptable answer. "I'm okay. I mean—"

My dad watches me. He knows he's being lied to.

And it occurs to me, my dad knows what it feels like to hurt someone badly. Maybe he could get what I'm feeling right now.

"I didn't like her very much," I say tentatively. "Chloe. She was kind of mean to me, if you want to know the truth."

My dad sits down on my green chair. "How so?"

I shake my head, a refusal to go there. "So I don't feel so sad that she died, but I feel . . . bad that I don't feel sad. Or—"

"That maybe it was your fault in some way," says my dad.

150

I look up, frantic to hear that this could not be my fault. I stare at him. "What do you mean?"

He shrugs. "Something awful happens to someone we didn't like, we become convinced we're somehow responsible. It's natural."

"What if you actually wished them dead?" I ask. I look over at my little crystal creatures. "Like, you asked the universe to make it happen?"

"You only asked the universe?" jokes my dad. "Not an actual hit man?"

"Can't really afford a hit man on my allowance," I say.

"Then I think you're in the clear."

I smile, wish I actually felt relieved.

Then my dad says, "Want to tell me what was going on with this girl?"

I should have expected this question. But I'm caught off guard. I can't tell my dad about Oliver. Cheating is just not something we can talk about. And also, if he knew, he might take back those magic words: "I think you're in the clear."

I wave my hand. "Just dumb who-likes-who stuff. Seemed like a big deal at the time."

My dad looks at me, waiting to see if he'll get any more. I keep the smile on my face. Thanks, Dad! All better now!

Finally, he stands up, says, "Okay, well, if you want to talk more, you know where to find me."

"Yup."

When he's gone, I look back at the computer screen, the empty box where I started to write my hateful thoughts. I hit refresh.

Instantly, more grief floods the screen. *We heart you forever, Chloe! We'll never forget you! I can't stop crying!*

There is no room for what I feel, no place I can say what I truly think.

I push away from my desk. I know for a fact I could post every single nasty thing Chloe did to me and people would go, "Why are you being so horrible? Why are you being so mean?"

I pace, buzzing with anger. I see my crystal animals on the sill. My dad's sweet little presents to his sweet little girl. I can't stand how ridiculous and childish they look.

My fingers reach, close on Phoebe the unicorn. With one monstrous swing, I hurl her across the room. She shatters against the wall; little chunks of glass land on my bureau, fall onto the rug. I knew she would break; I wanted to break her. But seeing her destroyed, I burst into tears.

Going to the bureau, I try to put her back together. Little Phoebe, my symbol of purity. With stupid, clumsy fingers, I push the shards into a pile, whimpering, "I'm sorry, I'm sorry, I'm so sorry. Oh, God, will you forgive me? Please?" Bits of glass cut my fingertips.

"I'm sorry," I say again to Phoebe's broken body. "I'm sorry. I know that doesn't mean anything, it doesn't fix it, but oh, God, I am so sorry."

CHAPTER TWELVE

THE NEXT MORNING BEFORE SCHOOL, I carefully peel the bandage from my hand. Today is going to be hell, and I don't want to draw attention to myself in any way. As it comes off, I see the blood, red and brown, on the white gauze. The cut is still raw and ugly-looking. A yellow crust of pus is forming around the edge. I wipe it with alcohol, feel the sharp sting of cleansing. Then I put a Band-Aid on.

The fact is, I will have a scar.

Yesterday, I thought there was no way I could go to school. But a numbness has settled in. I feel like someone could come right up to me and scream in my face, "You killed Chloe! You did it!" and I would just say "Yeah" in a lifeless voice. I don't feel good about that. Or righteous. I just don't feel. If caring is water—nourishing, life-bringing—I am sun-bleached bone.

I meet Ella on the corner. Her eyes are red, her face blotchy. When she sees me, the tears well. "God, I'm sorry," she says, wiping them away.

"What for?"

"I don't know," she says miserably. "Crying for someone who was so awful to you."

"Oh, God, Ella," I say tiredly. "There is no right thing. Feel what you feel."

As we start walking, she says, "Just, I've known her since second grade, you know? And I just can't believe—it's like, no, we'll get to school and she'll be there."

Wouldn't that be nice, I think.

Ella says, "Only she won't, and that's so hard to get my head around."

I want to be a good friend to Ella, but I find myself tuning out. Wondering things like, Will Chloe come back to haunt me? Will her spirit follow me forever? In a world where feelings can kill, it seems entirely possible.

Chloe will haunt me, I think. Maybe not as some ghostly apparition going *Woo, woo!* But what happened to her will always be part of who I am, something I've done. I wanted her gone; now she'll never be gone.

Then I hear Ella say, "The funeral's tomorrow afternoon. Are you going?"

"I don't know," I say, meaning absolutely not.

"Really?" Ella bites her lip. "It kind of seems like the thing to do."

"The funeral will be for her family and friends," I say. "I'm neither."

"Right. Right." Ella nods. "Would you . . . ?"

"What, Ella?"

In a rush, she asks, "Would you mind if I went? I know Chloe was totally evil to you, and I do hate her for that."

"Whatever."

"But I don't know, I kind of want to say good-bye? They're having it at that big church on Fifty-Third and Lex, near where we took test prep. How weird is that?"

I manage to respond, "Yeah, weird."

"So I would like to go? But only if it's okay with you. I don't want you to feel like I'm taking Chloe's side or anything."

I stare at her, amazed that she can still be caught up in sides and who likes who and who's whose friend. I want to scream, We're talking about a funeral, because Chloe is dead. She's dead because of me. So if you liked her at all? You should hate my guts.

"You should go," I say. "You cared about her. Honor that."

"But I feel like Chloe doesn't deserve for me to care about her," says Ella.

"Forget that. Honor that you care at all," I tell her. "Honor that your heart works."

As we approach the school, I see kids standing in large groups out on the street. Kids are crying, holding one another. Others are just sharing what they know in anxious, hushed voices. Inside, it's more of the same. Even the shy, out-of-it kids who had no reason to love Chloe are hushed and sad-looking. It's just as Cassandra predicted. Everyone is united in their grief.

I leave Ella with a small pack of Chloe mourners, then hurry upstairs to find someplace to hide. I never should have let Cassandra talk me into coming to school today.

I will not pretend to care, I want to scream. She was horrible. She beat me up. She hurt me.

Our grade spends all morning in assemblies and small groups, talking about what it means that Chloe is dead. We are reminded that drinking is bad. That if you do drink, take a cab. Or better yet, stay where you are.

I spot Cassandra in the hallway as she trails a group of the grieving out of the science lab. She's alone, her face unreadable. Clearly, she hasn't joined the sob fest—but it doesn't look like she's judging it either. I can't believe how calm she is. For a split second, I want to run to her side, say, I can't deal, tell me what to say, tell me how to look. Then I remember that today of all days, I cannot be linked to Cassandra.

I can't tell: Are people angry with me all over again because Chloe's dead? Or was she so crazy these past few weeks, people have a little sympathy for me?

Reality check: probably nobody's thinking about me today.

When I see Wallace Laird in math, I dare to say, "Kind of a crazy day, huh?"

"Sad day," he says. Then he looks at me. "Although maybe not for you."

I shred the corner of a piece of paper on the table. "This doesn't make me happy, Wallace."

He nods, but I can tell he doesn't believe me. Then he says in a broken voice, "She was so *tiny*—" and all of a sudden, I see the truck, powered by all my hate, rushing toward this girl.

Mr. Alistair coughs, his sign that he wants to start class. I raise my hand, ask if I can have a bathroom break.

That afternoon, I see Isabelle coming out of Ms. Petrie's office. Her dark hair hangs loose over her face, and her long, super-skinny body looks disjointed, as if screws have fallen out at her hips and shoulders. When she says thank you to the counselor, her voice is raw with crying.

I am struck by a memory of me pretending to walk out of Ms. Petrie's office so that Chloe would think I had reported her. By accident, I catch Isabelle's eye. For a moment, we just stand there, staring stupidly at each other.

Another memory comes back.

Gee, Isabelle, last time I saw you, you were slamming my head in a toilet. How's things?

Only Isabelle didn't do that—I remember now. It was mostly Zeena, gleefully carrying out Chloe's orders. Isabelle stayed away from that part.

Didn't do much to stop it, though.

Without her grinning hyena pack, she looks quieter, nerdier. She opens her mouth to say something. But then she stops as Zeena comes to collect her. For a second, Isabelle's eyes move back and forth between me and Zeena.

Who you gonna choose, honey child? pops into my head.

Zeena grabs Isabelle's arm, pulls her away.

Finally, the day is over. I decide I will go home, take the hottest bath ever, and find the dumbest thing to watch on TV. I will turn off my phone, close my door to my parents. In my altered state, I have the notion that if I never talk to anyone who knows me again, maybe I can become a totally different person.

A few blocks from school, I see a tall, dark boy standing on the corner ahead of me. He's wearing a winter coat, and I don't recognize him right away. Then I do, call out, "Oliver?"

He turns and sees me. For a moment we just stand there. He looks awful, like a ragged ink sketch in his black coat, black hair, and glasses. His skin is pasty, making him appear as if he's been carved out of old wax. He's clearly in pain. Things have been so messed up between him and Chloe and now they'll never be right. As weak and stupid and hurtful as he's been, I feel for him.

There has to be a reason the universe put him right in front of me. I must be meant to help him in some way. I open my mouth, ready to say . . . what, I'm not sure.

But before I can say anything, Oliver shakes his head, starts walking away from me. Desperate, I say, "Oliver . . ."

"No," he yells, not even looking at me. "No, I—"

He walks faster, as if I'm going to chase him. At the far corner, he turns, disappears behind a building.

"Okay," I breathe, trying not to cry. "Okay."

Then in my head, I hear, *Come be with me. Forget them. You're beyond them.*

And like Oliver, all I can think is no. I don't want to be with Cassandra right now. She's so sure what we did was right, and I'm not. I don't know if I ever want to be sure.

I turn to go home, but, by following Oliver, I've gotten turned around. I'm not sure: Should I go home? I really don't want to. There's too much I can't tell my parents right now.

I can't go back to school.

Can't go to the park, it reminds me of Cassandra and our spells.

I can't go anywhere. I don't belong anywhere.

This year in Western Lit, we started reading the Bible. In the beginning, all these people get exiled—like Adam and Eve getting thrown out of Eden, Cain getting banished after he murders Abel. I remember thinking, Is that it? Why doesn't God smite them down or whatever? How bad could banishment be? So you can't ever go back to where you were—big deal.

Now I know better.

* * *

The next day, I tell my mom I'm sick and I can't go to school. She thinks I'm not telling the truth about the first part but suspects I am about the second. In fact, both parts are true. I end up sleeping through most of the morning, a half sleep where memories of Oliver in the diner, Chloe's face as she circled me in the hallway, nasty laughter in the cafeteria, are swallowed up in the choking smoke from Cassandra's incense.

Then, around one o'clock, I open my eyes. I can't lie still another second. I have to get up, have to get out.

I take a shower. Get dressed. Drink three cups of coffee and eat two bowls of cereal.

For no good reason, I look at the clock. Chloe's funeral is at four o'clock.

It's three-fifteen now.

I had absolutely no intention of going to Chloe's funeral. I told Ella I wasn't going. I'm certainly not dressed for a funeral. And yet here I am on a bus headed to the east side.

This is wrong on just about every level, I tell myself. Someone's bound to get all righteous and slap me in the face for stealing Oliver. And I'm so brilliant, I'll probably retaliate by shouting, "Yeah, and I cut myself and burned things! That's why she ended up under that truck, ha, ha!"

They say you go to funerals to pay your respects. I have no respect for Chloe.

So why am I going?

159

The memorial service is at St. Sebastian's Church at Fifty-Third and Lexington. I know this neighborhood pretty well. It's a mix of old and new, with the sleek, silver Citicorp building soaring over stodgy old hotels and churches. Ella's parents and mine realized at about the same time that neither of their daughters was going to ace the SATs without major help. So last spring, they insisted we do test prep. At which point, Ella and I decided test prep would be utter and complete torture without a bud, so we insisted they send us to the same class. I don't remember a lot about the classes; mostly I remember laughing with Ella over Pinkberry afterward, about how low we were going to score and how we'd probably end up behind the Pinkberry counter serving snotty kids like us our whole lives. I remember Ella saying, "Well, *you* won't. But I will."

"You will not," I said.

"No," she said sadly. "This morning, I was trying to tell my dad about Gordon Ramsay's new show and he was like, I don't know this person and I don't care. And I don't know why you do. I was like, Oh, uh. Whatever the brilliance gene in my family is, it skipped me totally."

"Well, so did the tight-ass judgmental gene," I said. But I could tell it didn't cheer her up.

By the time I arrive, the service has already started and the heavy wood doors are closed. There's a little entry hall between the inner and outer doors. The walls and ceiling are cool gray stone, and the space feels slightly like a crypt. I pace, trying to figure out whether to go in. There are stacks of church bulletins in a wire rack. A little stone fountain is set into the wall. I look closer, see there's water in it, but no spout. Not a fountain. Holy water.

You sprinkle it on yourself and it protects you from evil spirits. Or it burns you if you are an evil spirit.

I have a terrible need to touch it. But stupidly, I'm scared.

A burst of organ music rattles the door. I crack it open slightly and peek in. The place is packed. Sobs ripple through the air. My stomach lurches. Chloe had a lot of friends.

I let the door close, wander back and forth across the stone floor of the lobby. I can hear the organ playing, slow and sad. I guess everyone's supposed to be thinking about Chloe now. I look up at the ceiling, wonder if she's floating up in the heavens. I imagine her kicking insufficiently fluffy clouds aside, going, "You want me to sit on that? No way!"

Maybe she's in hell. This is, after all, the girl who said, "First the bag, now the bitch." There was a hard-core meanness to Chloe. She could be cruel, got off on it, in fact. And it wasn't like she had any excuse. As far as I know, her life was pretty okay.

Except of course for the fact that it's over.

"And now—" The priest's voice jerks me back to the service. I crack the door again and see two women—no, a woman and a girl—making their way to the podium. They're both in black, and the woman has her arms tight around the girl. The woman is severe-looking, her dark hair pulled back like Chloe's. Chloe's mom—or maybe an aunt, because this woman has it too together to have just lost her daughter. The girl is maybe ten. She's sobbing into a handkerchief.

As she steps up to the lectern, you can hear her sniffling and choking. Finally, she manages, "Hi, I'm Chloe's sister, Amelie." Her miserable little-girl voice goes right through my gut like iron. I had no idea Chloe had a sister. And all of a sudden, it doesn't matter if Chloe was nice, not nice, what she did to me. This child is broken-hearted that her big sister is dead.

I turn, push the doors open, and go outside. Here it's bright, sunny. Chilly. The honking of cars, the rumbling of garbage trucks. People walking their dogs, sipping coffee as they go.

This is life, real life. No magic here. I lean against the cold hand-rail on the steps, take comfort from the cold, hard metal. I'll wait for Ella. Maybe we can go to Pinkberry after.

"Hey."

I turn, see Isabelle. Her brown hair is pinned back with a bar-rette. She's wearing all black. The way she's standing, moving her foot along the step, looking at me, not looking at me—I get the sense she knew I was out here. That she came to see me. She looks so uncomfortable, I know I have the power.

She points to the steps. "Mind if I sit down?"

I wave at the other end of the step. "Go ahead."

Isabelle sits, rearranging her skirt under her. "God, it's cold."

"That's what happens in October."

"I just couldn't be in there anymore." Then, keeping her eyes focused ahead, she says "For the record?"

"Yeah?"

"What we did to you was shitty." She says it all in a rush, like she has to get it out before I stop her.

She looks at me when she's done.

I say, "Sorry—did you want me to argue with you?"

"Guess not."

That's all I'm going to give her right now. And yet she stays.

"Just being in there"—Isabelle nods to the church—"you kind of start thinking about . . . soul stuff. Right and wrong."

"I know what you mean," I say, thinking of my terror at the holy water. If it feels good, I am a good person. If it stings, evil. If only it were that easy.

Then Isabelle says, "I started adding up all the things I felt guilty about." She laughs unhappily. "The list got too long, so I stopped."

Curious, I ask, "What else was on the list?"

"Well, you were at the top," she says. "But right after that"—this she has to say to the steps—"was letting Chloe walk home alone that night."

So—I am not the only one who feels guilty over Chloe's death.

"Come on, you couldn't know what was going to happen." I wonder who I'm absolving here—Isabelle or myself.

Isabelle shakes her head. "I should have known. She was a total wreck—ever since school started. And it wasn't getting better with time. You probably heard about the cafeteria thing."

I nod.

Isabelle continues. "Her parents put her on chill pills after that. But they obviously didn't work. Or maybe they made her more crazy, who knows. Plus, I'm sure you know . . ."

I'm not sure what she means, so I shake my head.

"Oliver breaking up with her? Because he supposedly wanted to get back together with you?"

"That's Zeena's story, not mine."

"Yeah, Zeen didn't do Chloe any favors spreading that around," says Isabelle bitterly.

"So she was freaking out."

"It was more than that. She wasn't thinking right." Isabelle blinks; tears run down her face. "She wasn't the Chloe I knew. Like she was hallucinating or something."

Or bewitched.

"What happened that night?" I ask.

Isabelle gives a big, shuddering sigh. "She was in a severely bad head space. Like, meds and vodka, probably not a great combo, right? Thank God Zeena wasn't there. She would've just made it worse. As it was, Chloe and I spent the whole night in a corner obsessing about—"

"Let me guess."

"She was convinced—don't take this the wrong way."

"I won't."

"She was convinced you were out to get her. She said you were stalking her at school. Even when you weren't around, she could supposedly feel you thinking about her. That night, she said she could practically hear you."

My curse shall haunt you, and my hate
No victim's blood shall expiate.

Isabelle says, "I told her, This girl is not thinking about you, *you* are thinking about her. And you need to stop. Because it's getting ridiculous and a little sick. If you want to be mad at anyone, be mad at Oliver." Isabelle drops her head. "Nice, right? The poor girl's been twisted in knots for months. And her supposed best friend screams at her to just get over it."

Tentatively, I say, "Well, maybe you had a reason."

"Yeah, sure. I was sick of hearing it. That was my big reason." Her mouth twists. "I just felt like you were all we were talking about. I thought once she and Oliver got back together, she'd be over it. No. So we sent you our little messages before school started. Did that stop the obsessing? No. We have to pull our crowd routine on you the first day of school. That's not enough. We have to convince the entire school that you're . . ."

She glances at me and I supply "A slut ho."

"Yeah," she says unhappily. "After a while, it was all we would talk about: how to get you. We spent hours making plans. At first, it was exciting. You know? In this very warped way. I mean, we always spent a lot of time bitching about people. But this time we were actually doing something. It made us feel . . . dangerous, I guess. Super cool," she says sarcastically. "God, we were such little bitches. Then one night, we were hanging out with Jackson, Zeena's boyfriend."

Hey, I got five minutes before class. Showing me his soft belly and hairy nipples.

Isabelle continues. "And he was like, 'Oh, you shoulda heard what I did to the slut today. She totally wanted to, man.' And Zeena and Chloe are laughing and giving him high fives, and I'm like, Uh, seriously? This is okay with you? By the way, Zeena, your boyfriend is scum? And I don't know, maybe we've all gotten a little scummy?"

When Isabelle says this, it all comes flooding back: Chloe's nastiness and viciousness, the way it felt like it would never end, that people wouldn't be satisfied until I had a total nervous breakdown.

And Isabelle has told me something else: Chloe was having fun.

Then Isabelle says softly, "The whole thing with the bathroom . . ."

"Yeah," I say. "What about that?"

"Well, you know, Zeena saw you talking with Oliver." Isabelle rolls her eyes, like, *Big crime.* "So she was totally hyping Chloe up. 'We have to do something big, we have to show her we're serious.' I was not into it. The whole thing was starting to creep me out. I thought for sure you'd go to the school and we'd all get kicked out."

"Did you ever say 'Uh, this is wrong? I'm not doing it'?"

"No," she says bitterly. "I just whined and said things like, 'Guys, are we sure we want to do this? We could get in trouble.' They just called me a weak-ass loser. Which I was, but not the way they meant."

We're quiet a while; then Isabelle says, "I tried to hold back. I don't know if that registered at all."

"A little." And that's all, I think.

Isabelle stares at her hands, folded in her lap. Then she says in a rush, "Anyway, I've been meaning to say if you want to go to the school now and tell them . . . what we did . . . I would go with you. I would totally admit to it and back you up in any way."

I was not expecting this, for Isabelle to actually offer to do something.

"Like you said, they'd kick you out," I tell her. "And Zeena. And I don't think Zeena would be too thrilled."

"I know. It'd be bad with Zeena and I'd have to deal with that. But for me?" She kicks at a piece of gravel on a lower step. "I almost want to be kicked out. I feel like it's what I deserve. I hate being in that building. I hate knowing I did those things. It makes me sick. Like, yeah, you think you're this basically nice person, but you're not. This is who you really are: a mean, spineless, shallow jerk." She looks at me, tears in her eyes. "I don't want to be that person. But I don't know how to get away from what I did."

My curse shall haunt you and my hate
No victim's blood shall expiate.

Isabelle starts to sob. I put my arms around her. But I don't know what to say or do. I can't undo what Isabelle did. And I can't undo what I did. All we can do is sit here and feel horrible.

Finally, Isabelle chokes out, "Well, gosh."

"Yup."

She sniffs, wipes her nose with her sleeve. "Now what do we do?"

I think. "Uh, say, 'Okay, that sucked. Let's not do that again.'"

Isabelle laughs. Then looks sad. "I just really, really wish I hadn't left Chloe alone that night. You know the last thing I said to her? When she was going on and on about how you hated her? I said, 'We did a terrible thing to her. No wonder she hates us. Stop being such a paranoid bitch.'"

Then shall mob, some future day,
Pelt you from street to street with stones,
Till, falling dead . . .

Isabelle says softly, "Alison made her promise to get a cab. She said she would, but—" She shudders. "I think she had decided, 'Let me step off the curb, let me not look, who cares? Nobody cares about me.'"

"It's not your fault," I say.

"You can't say that."

"Yes, I can," I tell her. "Yeah, you could have done things differently, but so could she and . . . so could I . . . and so could all of us." I fall silent, then finish, "But we didn't, and this is how it is."

Isabelle nods. Glancing back at the church, she says, "I don't want to go back in there."

"Then don't."

She stands up. "I meant it, what I said about going to the school. I want to make this right."

I don't know how to tell Isabelle that might not be possible, that we may have all gone too far for that. So I say, "Can I think about it?"

"Yeah, of course. And if you ever want to talk more"—she waves her hand awkwardly—"that'd be cool with me. Also totally understand if you don't."

"Okay."

"Okay. Well, see you."

" 'See you' back," I say.

When she's gone, I sit for a moment. I remember the time Chloe came over to my house when we were doing the history thing. I put out a plate of cookies, and her eyes went wide. I said, "I need a major butter-sugar boost to kick-start the brain."

She took one cookie out of politeness. I think she ate half of it.

When she left, she said to me, "God, you're lucky."

I was like, Luck? What? Excuse me?

"You can eat that stuff and it doesn't count."

I realized she meant the old bod. Embarrassed, I said, "Ah, check out the butt. You'll see where it goes."

She shook her head. "I could never get away with that in a million years. I'm that kind of person. Unless I totally keep it together, it all falls apart."

I realize now, I had Chloe wrong. She always seemed so powerful to me, but Isabelle was telling the truth when she said Chloe was scared. I could see it when I laid the hex on her. She was losing Oliver, losing the respect of kids at school, maybe even getting expelled. I could make her feel weak because she felt weak already. One wrong move and that would be it for her. No wonder she freaked out so bad over that stupid history project. No wonder she turned everything into a war. That's what life felt like for her.

Ah, Chloe, I think. You should have eaten more damn cookies.

Mourners are starting to come out of the church. I am not the first person people should see, so I go down the block to wait for Ella. If she's with people, I won't press it. But if she's alone, she might want company.

Ella is easy to spot with her bubble hair and Scream bag. She hurries down the steps. No one follows. Her head is down; she seems lost in her thoughts.

I tap her on the shoulder as she passes by. She glances up, seems confused. "Hey. Were you inside? I didn't see you. . . ."

"I stayed out here. But I thought maybe you'd want some company."

"Oh, that's sweet." She looks around nervously. "Are you with Cass?"

"No," I say, puzzled that she would ask.

Ella nods to herself. Then in a dark, bitter voice that sounds nothing like her, she says, "Right—why would *she* come?"

For an instant, I feel terrified that she knows absolutely everything that's gone on between me and Cassandra. Then I remind myself: Ella and Cassandra may be cousins, but they do not get along. That's all that is.

"Come on," I say, straining to keep my voice light. "I thought you might be in the mood for Pinkberry."

CHAPTER THIRTEEN

PINKBERRY IS FUNNY. IT ALWAYS makes me think of a dollhouse, with the pink walls and the white plastic tables and chairs. I feel like I should be ten years old when I'm there.

I get regular doused with strawberries. Ella gets the same, only with chocolate chips. We sit and I wait for her to burst out talking. Normally, Ella would be full of details about a big event like this. "Oh, my God, so-and-so was freaking out, I felt so bad for her." "I could not believe when so-and-so said this and that."

But she doesn't say a word. Instead, she concentrates on scraping the chips off the side of her yogurt, as if it's the only truly important thing in the world right now.

There are two kinds of silence. The "I have no idea what to say" kind and the "I have something to say but I'm scared to say it" kind. This feels like the second kind.

I have the hideous sense Ella knows what I did and she's afraid to look me in the eye. The longer we sit, the guiltier I feel. As if

Chloe's ghost rose at the funeral and whispered to Ella, "To-o-ni, To-o-ni did this to me."

Then I think, Stop being such an egomaniac. Ella's just been to a funeral of a girl she's known her whole life. Of course she's freaked out and upset. But she doesn't know how to say that without sounding like she's siding with Chloe.

I tell her, "You can talk about the funeral, I don't mind."

"No, it's okay," she says in a listless voice.

She carefully digs a single chip off the top of her yogurt, nibbles it; it's an old dieting trick. Make it last longer so you feel like you've eaten a lot.

Then, suddenly, she sticks the whole spoon in, pulls up an enormous bite of yogurt, and swallows it. She grimaces as it goes down, as if it hurts her throat.

"Pinkberry has to be allowed," I say. "It's yogurt, good for you."

"I don't know," she says fretfully. "I don't feel like anything's allowed."

"Ella, really. It's all right. I came to be here for you. Talk, already."

She looks at me, not sure I mean it. "It just—"

I nod encouragingly. "It just."

Ella hesitates. Then she blurts out, "I don't know, I guess I never saw anyone dead before."

"Must be so hard."

She kneads her forehead with the heel of her hand. "Not that I *saw* her, it was just the coffin, but . . ."

"Sure."

She glances at me. There's something else she's feeling, we haven't hit it yet. I stay quiet, determined to let Ella talk.

And she does, finally. "I was late, of course. So I ended up sitting right near Chloe's family." She pinches the bridge of her nose. "Oh, my God . . ."

This is part of my punishment, I tell myself. Having to hear what Chloe's loss means to people. "They're pretty destroyed, huh?"

Ella's eyes pop open. "Her little sister never stopped crying. You could hear it all over the church. All these . . . I guess cousins? Tears down their faces. Shoulders shaking. And her mom was a drugged-out zombie. I don't know what they put her on. Her dad looked like he wanted to *kill*. He kept clenching and opening his fists. His face was like this." She makes her jaw rigid, sinks her teeth into her lower lip.

"Oh, man. That's really hard."

"It was, it was hard. I felt totally useless. I kept thinking that because I was near them, I should do something for them. I know what they're going through, right? Someone in my family died. I've been through this."

"Right."

"But I couldn't think of anything to do or say. I felt like such an idiot."

"Oh, Ella."

She shakes her head abruptly. "But that's when I realized."

"What?"

"I actually haven't been through this."

I shake my head. "I lost you."

Ella's hands flap in the air. "No, just . . . when I saw Chloe's family, how wrecked they were, how they were putting their sadness right out there, because they couldn't help it? I realized, Oh, this is what a normal family looks like. Normal people actually *admit* when they're sad. It really made me think about my family. And how we are *totally* not dealing."

Careful because I don't want to shut Ella down, I say, "But you didn't go to Eamonn's funeral, right? You didn't find out until you came home."

"Right!" Suddenly, she's all fierce. "I was at Costa del Porco, and my mom was worried Eamonn's death would be a 'stress trigger.' Like I would shove a whole Entenmann's into my face if I knew. Right away, there was a whole secrecy thing going on."

"Well—or your parents are control freaks when it comes to your weight."

"Okay, but even now." Ella leans forward. "Even now, nobody's talking. Eamonn's name *never* comes up. My whole family's like, Oh, yeah that happened—but don't talk about it. There's no crying. No, Oh, my God, we miss him. Everything's so-called normal, except my aunt and uncle are like—" She widens her eyes and sways like the walking dead.

I think of Cassandra's mom that day I met her, how it felt like she was going to fall apart any second. "Maybe it's just too difficult," I say helplessly.

"Maybe," says Ella. "Or maybe nobody wants to talk about it because we're all thinking the same thing and not saying it. Maybe it's because—"

But then she stops. Taking up her napkin, she starts to shred it.

"Because what?" I ask.

Wiping her mouth with the shreds, she mutters, "Forget it."

"Say it."

"No, you're her friend now, I forgot."

Her friend. So all this is about Cassandra.

"I'm your friend too," I remind her.

Ella looks into my eyes, as if checking whether I'm telling the truth.

"I know," she says quietly. "I didn't mean it like that. But you shouldn't say not-nice things about people to people's friends."

I open my mouth to say, "Ella, it's *allowed*."

But Ella cuts me off, saying brightly, "Let's do something else. Let's do . . . *Top Chef*." She flaps her arms in pretend exasperation. "I was so pissed Carly got eliminated!"

I don't want to talk about *Top Chef*. I want to know what Ella was going to say about Cassandra.

But Ella doesn't want to talk about Cassandra. And I tell myself that right now, I am about what Ella wants. So we talk about TV and forget real life, and for a while, you could almost believe everything was back to normal.

It's dark by the time we leave. We roll through Central Park on the crosstown bus. Ella turns her head to watch the trees, all shadow as we fly by.

"You know what's weird?" she says dreamily.

"A million things?"

"I've never seen her cry."

Confused, I ask, "Who? What do you mean?"

"Cassandra." She turns, looks at me. "I've never once seen her cry for Eamonn. Supposedly, she loved him so much—why doesn't she cry?"

"I'm sure she did at the funeral," I say.

Ella looks out the window. Almost to herself, she says, "I'm not."

I drop Ella off at the corner where we part. As I'm walking the rest of the way to my house, my phone rings. I dig it out of my pocket. It's Cassandra.

I'm about to answer, but I hesitate. We'll end up talking about the funeral. I'll tell her I didn't go, but I sort of did. I'll tell her I talked to Isabelle, walked home with Ella. . . .

And she won't be pleased. By any of it.

The phone stops ringing.

Much later, I get up the nerve to listen to Cassandra's message. "Hi, I don't know why, but I'm having this weird feeling you went to the funeral today. So, I'm just calling to find out . . ." There's a big sigh. Then: ". . . you know—where you *are*."

"So, how was it?"

The next day, Cassandra and I meet after school. That's how Cassandra starts: "So, how was it?" asking about Chloe's funeral in a quick, offhand style that means *I know you went, so let's get this out of the way.*

We are sitting on a park bench on the path that winds around the rocks and into the Eighty-Third Street playground. Somehow, neither of us wanted to go to the rock; we both seemed to feel it was time for a change. Only we're not sure how big the change should be—or why we feel that way—and it's making us nervous. Our rhythm is off. I keep trying to find the beat of what Cassandra says, get a sense of how she's feeling. But she's all jumpy and zigzaggy, and it's hard to follow her.

I say, "It was sad. From what I saw. You know . . ." I shrug.

"I'm still not sure why you went."

I hesitate. Any mention of guilt over Chloe is a criticism of Cassandra. So I try, "Ella sort of wanted me to."

"Repeat: *not* sure why you went."

I want to say, Because we did a terrible thing, Cassandra. I needed to face up to what we did—a little tiny bit.

I say, "Yeah, I'm not sure either. It made sense at the time."

"Why did she want you to go?" Cassandra, I notice, rarely says Ella's name.

"For support. She was upset."

Cassandra leaps on this. "Oh, because Ella had to deal with *two* funerals? Poor Ella—no doubt she'll eat New Jersey to make herself feel better."

A warning bell goes off inside me. There is some intense weirdness in this family around Eamonn's death.

Struggling, I say, "I guess."

"Ella didn't even *go* to Eamonn's funeral, you realize that."

"She wanted to; her parents didn't even tell her until she got back."

"Oh, right." Cassandra throws herself backward. "What, she's whining that she didn't get to go? Saying how much she cared? Because she didn't, believe me—"

Cassandra's like a train, gaining speed, charging toward Ella, ready to wipe her out.

Trying to slow her down, I say, "That's not what Ella said at all—"

"So she *was* talking about Eamonn."

"She—" Confused, wanting to help Ella and Cassandra, I say, "She just wants to be there for people."

"So what's stopping her?"

"She feels like your family won't talk about it. Like it's this big . . . forbidden subject."

Something—maybe the word "forbidden"—catches Cassandra's attention. Turning on me, she asks in a low voice, "Did Ella say things about me?"

"No, Cassandra!" I lie. "Seriously."

Her gaze is still on me.

"We mostly yakked about *Top Chef*," I tell her.

Cassandra rolls her eyes. "Her pathetic obsession with food shows. How's that diet of hers going? I bet she's too 'stressed' to stick to it."

I don't touch that one. Cassandra bitching about Ella's eating is better than Cassandra demanding answers.

Cassandra lets it go—sort of, settling back and glaring at the world in front of her. I pull myself in, huddle down into my coat. It's cold. Why did we decide to be outside?

Wanting to get off the subject of Ella, I say, "Guess who I talked to at the funeral? Isabelle."

"What the hell did she want?"

"She was nice. She said she'd be willing to go to the administration, tell them what's been going on."

"I hope you told her to join her friend in the morgue."

This is too flip, even for Cassandra. I say, "Come on."

She stares at me. "What?"

"I don't want to joke about—it." I shrink inside my coat again. "It's not funny."

"Oh, God." Cassandra stretches her full length against the back of the bench. "Please don't tell me you still have the guilts. What, you think if you become besties with a single-celled amoeba like Isabelle, that's going to make what we did to Chloe—"

"Jesus, Cassandra!"

"—all better? Get a grip."

I look at Cassandra. Half of me expects to see a murdering psycho. But I just see a girl like me. Her face is flushed, her hair's blowing every which way, her hands are pushed deep into her pockets. She's fierce, upset—and alone. Furious that people are talking behind her back and she has no power to stop them.

I remember when Cassandra's fierceness made me feel sane. When the whole world decided I was a whore, when my parents were lost in their own craziness, when Ella was just . . . Ella, Cassandra was the only one who said, "Hey, this isn't right. You don't deserve this. Let's do something about it."

That counts. That matters.

Cassandra looks at me, her big eyes searching my face. I know she's asking, Are we actually friends? Or did you just kind of use me and now you don't need me anymore?

I kick her foot gently. "Why don't we try some happy magic? Love spells? Smart potions? Some good old-fashioned giggle juice?" When she doesn't answer, I add, "Now that the enemies are all gone."

In a distant voice, Cassandra says, "Yeah, right."

Later, as we're leaving the park, she says, "Tell me again."

"What?"

"What Ella said."

It's a test. I take a deep breath. "Only that she wishes you would talk to her. If you want to. She feels bad she wasn't there when it happened. Like . . . nobody trusts her enough to tell her the truth."

Cassandra stops, looks at me. "What truth is that?"

Stumbling, I say, "About . . . how they feel." Cassandra narrows her eyes. "For real. She feels left out of the family, that's all."

There's a long pause. Cassandra finally says, "Okay."

But her eyes stay on me.

When I get home, I have an impulse to call Ella and give her a heads-up that I told Cassandra she feels left out of the family.

No, that's not what I want Ella to know. It's that I told Cassandra that Ella talked to me about Eamonn.

Then I think, This is ridiculous. Why shouldn't Ella talk about Eamonn?

What will be, will be, *que será, será*, et cetera, I tell myself. My job is to just try and stay out of it.

At school, there are still flowers and cards massed in front of Chloe's locker. Her picture is still up in the entrance. Kids still start crying in class and have to be excused. In science, Noah Bergstrom asks for a moment of silence in Chloe's memory.

Ella is struggling in Spanish and so am I. So one day, we decide to struggle together after school. As I wait for Ella to pull what she needs from her locker, I hear Kendra Fargate pseudo-whisper to Dahlia Capshaw, "Wonder how long before she goes after Oliver?"

Dahlia says, "Did she ever *stop* going after Oliver?"

Ella turns, opens her mouth, but doesn't say anything.

I give her a little shake of the head: *Don't bother.*

As we head downstairs, she says helplessly, "I'm sorry."

"For what?"

Ella keeps her eyes on the steps as she makes her way down. "I wish I wasn't always so scared. I wish I could stand up to people. *Say* things that need to be said. Not be this terrified, quivering jelly thing."

I smile. "How are you this quivering jelly thing?"

Ella struggles, then says, "You know that show *Real Interventions?*"

"Um, no."

"It's seriously good, you have to watch. They take addicts, alcoholics—people who are totally destroying themselves. And their families and friends sit them down and say, Okay, here's the deal: You're going to die if you keep going like this. You would not believe how hard it is for these families to do the confrontation thing. You know they've felt this way forever, but they've been too scared to say anything. When they finally do speak up, it's like they're . . . hurling truth out there."

"Wow."

"I was watching it last night, and I was thinking, Why can't I do this?" She looks at me. "You know?"

"Tell people they're going to die?" I joke.

"No, like with my family, I feel like I'm such a wimp—"

Below us, I hear, "*What* about our family?"

Cassandra is standing at the foot of the stairs. Ella stops dead in her tracks. So do I. Cassandra looks from me to Ella, from Ella to me. Not unlike a cobra deciding where to strike.

"You were saying something about our family?" Cassandra prompts.

"N-n-no," stammers Ella. "Just, you know—I'm the family dummkopf." She fake laughs a little, can't keep it going.

Cassandra nods once: *Ah, yes.* Then she looks at me, the question clear on her face: *So, why are you hanging out with the family dummkopf and not with me?*

She's trying to make me choose, make it us against Ella. Or else her against the both of us. But I'm tired of enemies and battles. To Ella, I say firmly, "You're not a dummkopf."

To Cassandra, I say, "Want to hang after school tomorrow?"

Cassandra stares at me and I know: what I repeated to her about Ella that day in the park has not been forgotten.

Glancing at Ella like she's a particularly revolting insect, Cassandra says, "Some other time." Then walks past us up the stairs.

When Ella and I get to my house, we go to my room and struggle with the infernal subjunctive. It's all but impossible to concentrate. As much as I don't want to get involved in the weirdness between the cousins, I can't stop thinking about what happened.

Ella must be fretting too, because she's even dizzier than usual. Finally, I call for a snack break. After setting out tea mugs and cookies on the dining room table, I say, "Question."

Ella takes a cookie, nibbles at the edge.

"What was all that in the hall with Cassandra?"

Ella looks evasive. "I don't want to put you in the middle."

"I'm already in the middle because I care about you both. What's going on?"

Ella doesn't say anything.

"I know you guys are very different, I know you're not besties, but it feels like you hate each other now. . . ."

Ella looks at me. "I don't hate her."

"But you think Cassandra hates you?"

She nods.

"Always?"

Ella shakes her head. "We were okay when we were little. I can remember going over to her house, her coming to mine. We actually played together."

"So what happened?"

"She's brilliant and I'm a fat dope?" I give her a warning look. "Part of it was Eamonn. She was eight when he was born, and once her parents realized there was a problem, they became all about Eamonn. I can remember my mom telling my aunt to remember she had two kids. But Cassandra could get real fierce about him too. When we were all together, she'd blame me a lot."

"Like how?"

She tilts her head from side to side as she remembers. "If he started having one of his fits, she'd be like, 'Ella did it! Ella bothered him.'"

"That's not great," I say.

Ella takes another cookie, pours milk in her tea. For a moment, I think that's all she's going to say.

She takes a deep breath and announces, "Then this really weird thing happened when we were eleven."

"What?"

"Our families had rented this house by a lake for the summer. One day, Cassandra dared me to try and swim out to the dock in the middle of the lake. She knew I wasn't a good enough swimmer. But I tried, because she was looking at me like, If you can't do this, you're this fat, gross thing and I won't play with you. And she was the only one around to play with, so . . ."

"So you tried?"

She nods.

"What happened?"

"I got exhausted, freaked out, and nearly drowned. My dad came just in time and pulled me out. Mucho drama, as you can imagine. But Cassandra just stood there, calm, no hassle. Even when I was in real trouble, flailing around in the water." She frowns.

She picks up her mug, takes a long drink. "I'd totally forgotten that until the other day."

"What day?"

"Chloe's funeral," Ella explains.

She waits. There is something Ella wants me to understand—but she doesn't want to say it out loud.

I try, "Yeah, Cassandra likes to play with the extreme."

"It's more than that," says Ella.

She picks up a pen, plays with it. "I know you're her friend, but can I ask a question?"

"Of course."

"Do you ever get scared of her?"

I know exactly what Ella means. But all I say is "Cassandra has this tough-chick act. Yeah, it's intimidating. But you can't take it seriously."

Ella watches me. I can tell she's not buying it.

I ask, "What are you saying, Ella?"

She doesn't answer. Instead, she picks up her Spanish textbook and says, "Can I tell you how much I hate the subjunctive?"

That night, I'm reading *The Grapes of Wrath* with my phone beside me on the bed. I'm supposed to have it off when I do homework. But uh, sometimes I forget.

I'm underlining a passage when I hear the *bloop* that tells me I have a message.

I check it out. It's from Cassandra.

What is she saying?

I stare at the screen, feeling deeply annoyed. At least Ella tried not to pull me into this craziness. Cassandra just takes it for granted that I'm in it—and totally on her side. I want to say, Dude, you have the power here. Stop, already.

I text back, *Uh, big doings on* Hell's Kitchen?

I hesitate, then add, *Chill, okay? It's not like she's out to get you.*

A few minutes later, Cassandra answers, *Isn't she?*

CHAPTER FOURTEEN

THE NEXT WEEK, I'M ON eggshells, wondering when things will flare up between the cousins again. But Cassandra sends no more texts and Ella's all caught up in her reality shows. Every Thursday morning, we talk *Top Chef.* Fridays, I get the *Project Runway* update, and of course, she tells me what's up on her new fave, *Real Interventions.*

At last, I find myself actually having small conversations with people about . . . dumb, normal stuff. Things like papers on *As You Like It,* SATs, and how if Ricky Nunez wasn't on our varsity soccer team, we wouldn't *have* a varsity soccer team. I still get looks and there are still people I avoid. But I start to think it might be possible to get my wish from the beginning of the year: to become a different person, one who never messed with Oliver or fought with Chloe. To finally put this summer behind me.

Of course, that girl wasn't friends with Cassandra. And I'm not sure how this girl will be. I miss her. I smile when I see her in the hallway, but she doesn't smile back. I can't help thinking she's freezing me out as a punishment for being friends with Ella.

One day, I spot Ella coming out of English class. It's almost lunchtime, so I catch up with her and say, "What's up, bubbeleh? What's the scoop?"

She looks up, smiles. "Oh, hey—"

Then the smile vanishes. Puzzled, I look behind me.

And see Cassandra.

I'm about to say, "Okay, hussies, let's play nice." But something in Cassandra's expression stops me. Her vibe is beyond cold, almost cruel. She doesn't even seem aware of my presence. She's staring straight at Ella. Who now looks like she's going to cry.

Cassandra says, "What did you say, Ella?"

Ella makes a funny noise in her throat. "I didn't say anything . . . I just . . ."

I look toward Cassandra, hoping for a clue as to what the hell's going on. But Cassandra keeps her eyes on Ella, hard and fierce.

It's a hex, I realize suddenly. She's working a hex.

I say, "Guys."

Cassandra glares at me. For a second, I hear her, just like I used to. *Whose side are you on?*

Then she fixes her gaze back on Ella. Ella lets out a sob and runs down the hall, hugging her backpack for protection.

To Cassandra, I say, "What the hell?"

"Ask her," she says, and walks away.

I race after Ella. It's lunchtime so the hallways are crowded. Murmuring, "'Scuse me, coming through," I catch up to Ella just before she reaches the stairwell.

I grab her arm. "Stop. Talk to me."

"I can't." She twists, tries to get free.

"You have to," I tell her. Ella's so freaked it isn't hard to guide her into the music room right down the hall. It's empty now, just music stands and stacked scores piled high on folding chairs. I shut the door, hear the soundproofing cut off the outside noise.

"Okay." I sit Ella on a folding chair. "What is going on?"

"N-n-nothing," stammers Ella, her eyes wide with panic.

"Ella!" I jab a finger toward the hallway. "What is going on between you and Cassandra?"

She shrieks, "Nothing! She just hates my guts, okay?"

I shake my head, rejecting that. "Things have been deeply weird with you two ever since Chloe's funeral."

And, I think guiltily, ever since I told Cassandra that Ella was talking about Eamonn.

Ella mumbles, "Ask her. Nothing's changed with me."

"That's not true," I say. "You've been obsessing about Cassandra and your family. Like when you said your family didn't act like Chloe's family, what did you mean by that?"

"Nothing."

"Why were you so hung up on whether Cassandra cried or not at Eamonn's funeral?"

"I don't remember."

I feel evil, like some awful lawyer beating up a little old lady witness. But I have to know.

"What were you talking about when you said everybody in your family was thinking the same thing but no one was saying it?"

Ella suddenly folds in on herself and wraps her arms around her head. For a few moments, she rests there. Then she sits up and says, "Just . . . I can't figure out what happened."

"When?"

"That night." She looks at me. "Why did Cassandra leave Eamonn alone that night?"

"She was there. . . ."

"No, in the bathtub. Why did she leave him in the bathroom?"

I pull up a chair next to her. "From the beginning."

She takes a deep breath. "Eamonn had a seizure, right?"

I nod.

"Well, that was their worst fear—my aunt and uncle. They were terrified that Eamonn would seize when they weren't there to help him. So you never left Eamonn alone. Not *ever*. Once, I went to the bathroom while he was watching television. My uncle went totally berserker on me. *You don't leave him alone! Don't you know what could happen? Never, ever leave him!* Like I'd handed Eamonn a box of matches and said, 'Get your groove on.'"

"What are you saying, Ella?"

"I'm saying . . . you can't leave him alone in front of the TV, but Cassandra lets him take a *bath* by himself? Brilliant Cassandra who never makes mistakes?"

She stares at me like, Do you get it now?

I do. She's accusing Cassandra of murdering her brother.

My dad would say this is what people do when tragedies happen: they look for a reason, someone to blame. But I know Cassandra feels terrible about Eamonn.

However—have I ever heard Cassandra say so? What has she actually said?

I was good at knowing what he needed. . . . In a way, I gave him what he needed.

My parents just left us alone one too many times.

No, I think, Ella is just scared of her powerful cousin—and maybe, just maybe, wants to get back at her for treating her like caca all these years. Ella thinks she's sincere, but really, she's just stirring up trouble. Bubble, bubble, toil and trouble. And I have had way too much of that.

"Ella, Cassandra feels horrible about Eamonn's death. I know this."

Ella shuts down. "Okay."

"I'm not saying you're crazy."

"No, I get it," she says distantly.

This is not agreement, it's interruption: *You don't know anything. Shut up.*

But I can't shut up.

"Ella, have you mentioned this to anyone else?"

Ella hesitates. "Not really."

I wait.

Then Ella sighs and says, "Okay. A few days ago, I watched that show I like—*Real Interventions.* And I thought, Well, you know, maybe it's time I stop being such a wimp and do an intervention with my own screwed-up family. I should let them know the truth for once. So later that night, I went to my mom—"

She breaks off, swallows hard.

"And?" I ask.

"And I said to her, 'Isn't it kind of weird Cassandra wasn't in the bathroom with Eamonn?'" Ella's voice is scared, but defiant.

"And?"

"Oh, she totally freaked out. At *me*—just like I knew she would. Started yelling, like, What are you saying and why would you think that? Did Cassandra say something?"

"What did you say?"

Ella bites her lip. "Nothing. When my mom freaked, I lost what little guts I had and totally backed down. I told her, Cassandra didn't say anything, it's just me being crazy, forget it."

"And did your mom forget it?"

Ella doesn't say anything.

"Or did she maybe talk to your aunt?"

Her eyes fill with tears. "Oh, God, do you think she did?"

It kind of seems like Cassandra wants to destroy you, I think. So, yeah, I think so. But I say nothing.

"I never thought she'd do *that*," Ella wails. "I thought she'd just . . . tell me what happened, you know? Oh, God, if she did that . . . Cass must seriously hate me."

I would like to tell Ella she's wrong, but I can't.

"What do you think she'll do?" whispers Ella.

I have no answer to that question. At least, none that would make Ella feel better.

As I'm leaving school, someone grabs me by the arm.

"Hello, madame," says Cassandra. "We're doing a survey on the subject of bilious blabbermouths and we'd like your opinion. Would you care to participate?"

I wouldn't—not at all. But I know Cassandra will destroy Ella if I don't talk her out of it.

We go to my house this time because it's closer. Luckily, my dad has late classes today.

"So—how was your week?" says Cassandra the second I close the door. She's pacing around the dining area, checking everything out.

"Uh, fine," I say.

"Uh-huh. Want to hear how mine went?"

"Sure."

"My parents and I had a little talk. Want to guess what it was about?"

"No."

"Therapy!" She shouts it. "Yes, family therapy!"

Slowing down, she ticks off the rest like a recipe. "Mom's suggestion. Dad agrees. We're not sure yet: her shrink or his. Or maybe a third party. Oh, and I'm invited. In fact, *I* am the guest of honor."

She grins manically, eyes shining. I say, "What, like grief counseling or something?"

"Hmmmm . . . sort of."

I need time to think about what this means, so I say, "Let's go to my room."

Cassandra has never been to my lair, but she immediately plops herself down at my desk. She has no interest in what's around her, she just focuses on me.

"She talked to her parents," she says bluntly. "That's what happened, I know it."

I have to pretend I don't have a clue. "Ella?"

"Yup." She spins in the chair. "Yup, yup, yup, yup, yup." Suddenly, she stops. "And then her mom called my mom and now—my mom can't look me in the face."

The chair spins again. "I'm going to kill her," she adds pleasantly.

I have to slow things way down. Sitting on my bed, I settle several pillows behind my back before saying, "I can totally understand—"

Cassandra interrupts. "By the way, *do* you know? What she's saying?" She peers at me.

I hesitate. "She has, in her goofy Ella way, been talking about Eamonn and your family. But I don't really listen. You know Ella. Everything's a drama. . . ."

"I knew it," says Cassandra almost to herself. "I knew it was her. She went yapping to her mom. Who then went yapping to mine."

I say, "Your mom just wants to see a shrink—"

"My mom sees a shrink every day. This is different."

"But just because—"

"No!" Cassandra gets up. "No, do not. Try to convince me that this isn't what this is. I know what that idiot is saying about me."

Cassandra's rage is so powerful it's like a roaring fire. Anything I say is just going to fuel it. I shake my head.

"She's saying I let Eamonn die, right? That I wanted him to die."

"No—"

"Oh, sorry," says Cassandra sarcastically. "She's *implying* it. Doing her little 'Gosh, isn't it kind of weird?' routine."

Okay, that is what Ella's doing. And I wish she weren't. But Cassandra is scaring me. I do not believe she hurt Eamonn. But I do believe she will hurt Ella. Badly.

"I don't think anybody takes Ella seriously," I say.

"My mom does. Believe it."

Your mom was worried before Ella, I think. I saw it in her face that day I met her. Maybe Ella's the only one saying it out loud. But your mom wondered too.

I say, "Then maybe the best thing is that everyone gets in a room and a doctor tells your mom she's crazy. She wants someone to blame, probably."

"Yes, she does—me," Cassandra rages. "Thanks, Mom." She wheels around. "I bet she's saying it all over school."

"I really don't think so," I say. "And since when do you care what people think about you?"

Cassandra stops instantly. "Excuse me? People think I let my brother die and I'm not supposed to care?"

She pauses.

"Why don't you talk to Ella?"

"About how she'd prefer to die?"

"Not funny, Cassandra. I don't think Ella understands—"

"'What she's doing, blah, blah.' You always think that."

"Because that's how most of us *are*," I say. "We hurt people, but we don't really know we're doing it or we don't know how bad it hurts."

I remember Katherine the moment she realized she had completely shattered my life with a few words she barely knew she was saying out loud.

"You said that yourself," I remind her. "That's why we should use our power over others *wisely*."

"And that's how I'm deciding to use it now. Ella's getting attention with this," says Cassandra harshly. "And the porky little blabbermouth won't stop until we make her stop."

There's the word I was dreading: "we."

"Just talk to her," I say weakly.

"No. Talking time is done."

I'm not going to hurt her, I tell Cassandra in my head. *I won't. Even if she tells everyone in school, spray-paints it on the gym floor, I'm not hurting her.*

"What do you . . . ?" I say.

"I'm not sure. I have to think about it." She pauses. "Are you in?"

You have to help me. I helped you. The words hang between us like a heavy smog—even a little whiff makes you sick.

Stalling, I say, "I want to hear what 'it' is."

"Okay. I'll think about it over the weekend. Monday, I'll tell you," she says.

The weekend, I think. That's how long I have.

Sunday night, I sit in my sweatpants and T-shirt and move my creatures around. Mimi has been standing with Aura for weeks; now I separate them, put each on opposite corners of the windowsill. Mimi is in shadow. But the streetlights hit Aura with a bright glare. I switch them. Mimi doesn't look happy in the harsh light. Or with being alone. Sorry, Meems, that's how it goes right now.

I still feel it, the little empty space that belonged to Phoebe. Being the crazy person I am, I swear the other animals are angry with me. They saw me destroy her. I wonder if they worry they could be next.

Guys, I won't do that, I think to them. No matter what happens, no matter how angry I get, I will never, ever hurt any of you again. I promise.

I go to bed. I don't sleep well. But at some point, I do wake up. And it's Monday.

Cassandra says as we climb up to the rock, "So then Ms. Kramer was like, Well, this isn't what I had in mind when I gave this assignment, and I said, Well, I can't help what you had in your mind. Like if you think I'm going to be ruled by that, you're loony-bin bound. And she said, Comparing Beowulf to Kurt Cobain isn't a real argument. And I said, Well, we're arguing about it now, aren't we? Just because her frame of reference is limited to things that occurred prior to 1970, we should all be ignorant. Makes me insane. . . ."

Nervous, I realize. Cassandra is actually nervous. Normally, she never discusses school. Teachers, classes, they're minor irritants in her day while she lives her real life elsewhere. But right now, school is the only safe thing to talk about.

"So what'd she say?" I ask. Cassandra's walking ahead of me, so I speak to her back. She doesn't answer right away, concentrating on those last few steps, which can be tricky because of the weird bumps and crevices.

She reaches the top. Turns around and looks down at me. I smile—*Just let me get there.*

And she says, "You're not going to help me, are you?"

I take the last big step. Out of breath, I plant my hands on my hips. "I will help you—"

"No, you won't." The wind catches her hair, whips it around.

"I *will*. Just not the way you wanted."

I would like to come off super strong as I say this. But instead, my chin falls to my chest, I stare at the ground.

"Ella deserves to be punished, you know that."

I gulp air, shake my head. "I don't want to punish anymore. Not after what happened to Chloe." Now I can look up. "I don't have that right."

"You don't have the guts," Cassandra says in a pleasant voice. "But I do."

I can't tell if she means the guts or the right. Maybe they're the same thing to her.

I try, "Doesn't it upset you, even the slightest bit, what happened to Chloe?"

"No." The shake of her head is immediate. "I really don't believe in false sentiment. Some people should not be on this earth. When they go, all you can do is say, Yeah, good. We're all better off."

"Well, I don't think we get to decide that," I say. "And I really don't think Ella deserves anything so extreme."

"Oh, well, that could be a problem."

"What do you mean?"

Cassandra shrugs as if it's obvious. "I'll have to go stronger if you're not helping me."

"Why?"

"Well, when you have the energy of two people, you can work a milder spell to better effect. Like that little silencer act we pulled on Oliver. If you or I had done that on our own, it probably wouldn't have worked."

She nods to herself. "So it'll have to be a powerful spell, I think. Too bad, I was kind of hoping to let Ella off with a sore throat, bad rash, something like that."

I can't tell if Cassandra's serious or not. Maybe this is a trick to get me to say, Oh, is that all you were planning? Sure, I can help with that.

But I don't trust her anymore.

"Why don't you just talk to her?" I try again. "I could come with you guys, be the peacekeeper."

"No," says Cassandra simply. "I don't want to make peace. I want to hurt her. The same way you wanted to hurt Chloe. The only difference is, I'm honest about it and you're chickenshit."

I'm almost grateful for the nastiness. It makes it easier to realize that our friendship is over.

"What are you going to do, Cassandra?"

"I really haven't decided," she says lightly. "So many fun choices. Ella's such a klutz, almost anything would be believable. Ooh!" Her eyes light up. "Maybe something with a bathtub. She slips, falls . . ."

"It's not funny."

"Who's being funny?" She takes a step toward me. There are still a few feet between us, but I back up. My heel lands lower than I expected: the rock slopes here. I throw out my arms for balance.

Cassandra takes another step. "It is amazing, isn't it? How many places there are to fall? So many insecure spots where the unexpected can happen."

Is there anything solid behind me? I don't dare look down.

I can't take my eyes off Cassandra, in case I miss a raise of her hand, a sudden lunge.

She just wants to scare you, I tell myself. Wants you to feel her power. Just like any bully.

"I'm not going to let you hurt Ella, Cassandra." I blurt the words out without thinking. As they fade into the air, I think, So melodramatic, for God's sake.

Cassandra's totally still. Then her hands slide into her pockets as she draws her body tight and compact.

"So it's war?" she says calmly.

"I—I'm not saying that," I stammer, knowing full well that I will lose any war with Cassandra. She's stronger than I am in every way.

"I want to do something, you want to stop me. That means war."

"I'm just saying," I tell her, trying to keep my voice steady, "that I'm not going to let you hurt anyone."

She rolls her eyes. "And what're you going to do? Tell Teacher?"

"I'll do what I have to," I say.

Her eyes gleam. "Really?"

"Yes."

"I'll win, you know. I am stronger."

I know. "We'll see."

She starts climbing down the rocks, her steps jaunty and sure. For a moment, she stops, looks back up at me.

"It'll be fun," she calls. Then trit-trots down the hill.

CHAPTER FIFTEEN

"FUN," I THINK ON THE way home. What will "fun" feel like? Will I wake up tomorrow and not be able to see? Or move? Will I wake up tomorrow at all?

What am I fighting here? I ask myself. What can Cassandra really do?

Whether the magic is real or not, Cassandra has power. Because anger has power.

She's going to attack Ella, obviously. She's already got the hex going, and it's working. Ella's frightened, feeling weak. Eventually, Cassandra will cast a spell. But what kind? And will I see it coming?

One thing I've denied her is a coven. Cassandra has told me spells are way more powerful when you work with others. She might say she can work a spell by herself, but the fact that she brought it up tells me she's not sure what the result will be.

If she does try to find an ally, who would she choose? I was Cassandra's only real friend this year. Ella is a natural target at our school, people do make fun of her and roll their eyes. Cassandra's an outsider, people think she's weird. She can't get someone else to pick on Ella the way Chloe used the whole school against me.

How does Cassandra think this war will be fought? If she sees this as a battle between two witches, how do we attack? How do we defend?

How do I win?

The next day, it hits as I walk into school, the gut-tightening feeling of terror I had at the beginning of the year. The knowledge that someone in this building wants to hurt me. I feel like Cassandra can sense that I'm here, she knows where I am. And when she's ready, she'll . . .

Okay, chill, chickarina. It's Ella, not you, who is Cassandra's target. And this is a school. Cassandra can't bring a truck into a school.

I used to be miserable that I had no classes with Cassandra; now, obviously, I'm relieved. No heavy textbooks dropped on my hand. No acids thrown in my direction. But I have no classes with Ella, either: I can't watch out for her.

I have study period before lunch, and I head to the library. Before now, the library was just a fun place to see if you could make out without anyone spotting you. Now I actually want to find a book. A very particular kind of book. Something that might help me fight a very powerful, pissed-off witch. I don't have time to write my own Book of Shadows. But Cassandra must have gotten her spells from somewhere. Maybe if I can find a book with the spells, I can learn how to beat them back.

I glance over at Mr. Hallows, the librarian. He's cool in a goony kind of way. But I don't see asking him if he has a witchcraft battle manual.

Witches, I think, letting my fingers trail over the books' spines. What do witches do? Where do they get their power?

The only books I find are on the Salem witch trials. I did a report on them in fifth grade, but all I really remember is a bunch of girls freaking out that witches were after them, and anyone who didn't go to church fifty million times a day was condemned to death, because hey, it was the sixteen hundreds and the Puritans were batshit crazy.

I open one of the books to an image of a young girl in a dark, heavy dress. She's rolling around on the courthouse floor, supposedly possessed. Behind her, other girls are screaming and pulling their hair out as they accuse their neighbors of casting evil spells on them. I wonder, was it all a game to them, a way to get at people they didn't like? Did they really talk themselves into believing witches were torturing them? Maybe some sixteen hundreds version of me and Cassandra were actually zapping them with evil energy.

I read:

> Some historians believe that those who claimed to be afflicted by witches may have been in the grip of mass hysteria in response to Indian attacks or other outside threats. Others point to motivations such as jealousy, spite, or the need for attention.

Chloe, I think, believing I was out to get her. Then I remember her fight with Hannah, her outrage when she couldn't control everything. And she convinced her friends that she was my victim. I remember how Chloe, Zeena, and Isabelle pinned me against the wall, the creepy way they moved as one, like zombies. *Must. Get. The. Slut.* Talk about mass hysteria.

Poor Princess Chloe, the evil slut out to get her.

Or the evil witch, I think. And let's be honest, we did get her.

Or did we? We got drunk and had a satanic slumber party. Chloe got hit by a truck because she was drunk and not paying attention. Alcohol, that's the big "magic" here.

But that's not all, I think uneasily. It's not that simple.

Looking back at the book, I think how weird it is that everyone believed these girls. No one said, Hold up, wait. Just because these chicks say they're getting pinched and poked by demons doesn't make it so. It's like people wanted to believe that their neighbors were evil, that they deserved to be hanged and burned and crushed. It's like, Aha—there's the danger! If we just stamp that out, everybody will be safe. If you get rid of the man-stealing slut, no one will get dumped by their boyfriend again.

Not to mention, people enjoy a good hanging. How much was happening in old Salem in the sixteen hundreds? Kind of fun to whip yourself into a frenzy and drag anyone who doesn't strike you as "your kind" to the hangman. How do you know you're righteous unless someone else gets pegged as a sinner?

All it takes is a few kids deciding another kid is creepy or lame or weird, and the whole school agrees. How many times do any of us say, "Hey, I like so-and-so," once the hex of unpopularity has been set? And if so-and-so gets teased or ignored or . . .

... gets her head shoved in the toilet ...

how many of us say, "Hey, not cool"?

Ella, meanwhile, is a nervous wreck. All her life, she may have felt Cassandra hated her—but now she knows it for sure. This does not make spending eight hours a day in the same building with her at all easy. So far, Cassandra has made no major moves. But the hex campaign is still going strong—and working, big-time.

On the walk to school, Ella says, "I'm terrified of bumping into her in the hallway. I can't even go to the bathroom."

"Just be happy you don't have classes or homeroom with her."

"Yeah, but the other day? I was in the cafeteria having lunch. Cassandra was sitting a few tables away and just ... staring at me. Like she was wishing I would choke. I couldn't even finish eating, she weirded me out so much."

She looks at me, hoping I have advice, something that can help her. I wish I did.

"Maybe once they get into therapy, this will all die down," I say.

"Maybe," says Ella doubtfully. "God, why did I have to say anything? Seriously, sometimes I think my life would be better in every way if I just kept my mouth *shut*."

Every day feels like a waiting game. I walk down the hallways wondering if I'll catch Cassandra doing ... what? I don't even know what I'm watching out for. Other than giving Ella the evil eye, Cassandra seems to be avoiding her. All I can hope for is that once her family starts the sessions, the grief and weirdness will ease up. Maybe one day, Cassandra will feel like Ella did her a favor.

And one day, maybe I'll be besties with Zeena.

Then one night, Ella calls me. She's crying.

"What?" I say. "What happened?"

"I'm scared," she says.

"Okay, I'm here. Why?"

I hear her sniffle as she tries to get it together. "Well, this weekend's my mom's birthday, right?"

"Uh-huh."

"And we always go out to dinner. To celebrate. Only this time, my mom says my aunt, uncle, and Cassandra are coming too."

"Oh, God."

"I don't know what I'm going to do. She says this is a time we should be together, like, support each other, and I'm like, Now? Now we have to do this?"

"Okay, calm down. Cassandra can't do anything to you in front of your folks."

"It freaks me out just to be in the same building as her. Imagine the same table. My stomach hurts."

"Just pretend she's not there."

"I feel her, I swear, even when I can't see her."

I have a nasty memory twinge of how Chloe said the same thing about me the night she died.

"Bring your phone and text me the whole time," I tell Ella. "That'll keep your mind off your family."

She laughs a little. "My mom would kill me."

"Well, better her than Cassandra."

* * *

Saturday night, I eat early, then go to my room and take up position on my bed. Ella said the dinner would start at seven. At six-thirty, I send her,

COURAGE!

Which must remind her of the Cowardly Lion because she texts back, *I do believe in spooks, I do believe in spooks.*

Quit it.

Text from Ella at 7:05. *Okay, this is 50 shades of hell.*

I text back, *I'm right here.*

At 7:12, Ella texts, *Bread's here, yay!*

I text, *Saved by the carbs!*

At 7:18, *Whoever invented mozzarella, I love you.*

I text, :)

7:23. *The waiter's hot. I think you'd like him.*

I type back, *Down, girl.*

Then at 7:26. *Oh, crap, they remembered I exist . . .*

I text COURAGE! again and set the phone down. If Ella's family is talking to her, it might take a while for her to answer me.

After ten minutes, I check the phone. Nothing from Ella.

I text, *Did you go off with that waiter?*

No answer. Obviously, Mom and Dad made her put the phone away.

At ten o'clock, I text, *Hey there. I need a weirdness update. How'd it go?*

No answer.

10:15. *Did you survive?*

Still not getting her.

10:34. *Ella, seriously. I'm worried. Give me a sign of life.*

But nothing comes.

* * *

On Sunday, I call. There's no answer.

Monday morning comes, and I race out of the house. When I see Ella standing on the corner, I feel bone-deep relief. Mom and Dad clearly flipped big-time and took her phone away for the weekend. That's why she couldn't text or call.

Normal survives, I remind myself. Normal is more powerful than you think.

I bounce up to her. "Hey, there!"

Ella says, "Hi" back. But her head is down, eyes away from mine. Her voice is quiet, withdrawn.

I prompt, "So?"

"Hm?"

"The dreaded dinner, how'd it go?"

"Oh." A dark ripple of memory across her face and she starts walking.

I press. "Was it okay with Cassandra?"

"Uh, yeah. It was fine."

"Well, good," I say, for lack of anything else.

I want to ask, What happened with the phone? Did you get in trouble? But there's something about Ella's expression that tells me questions are not welcome.

I'm trying to think of a way to say, Ella, I can tell something happened, when she says abruptly, "Sorry, I'm just really not up for talking this morning."

Then she reaches into her bag and pulls out some earphones.

Putting one in each ear, she tunes me out for the rest of the walk. She doesn't even take them out when we get to school, giving me a little wave good-bye as she heads up the steps.

It's started, I think.

Later, I ask Ella if she wants to have lunch.

She hesitates. "I have a major exam coming up. I should use the time to study."

"You can't think on an empty stomach."

"I brought my lunch."

"Oh—cool."

I try again the next day, but she says the same thing: she has to study. Half joking, I say, "Okay, where's the real Ella? What have you done with her?"

"Maybe I'm trying to change a little bit," she says, and walks away.

It's important to stay close to Ella, and I can't do that if we fight. So for the next few days, I act completely clueless that she's . . . well, avoiding me. One afternoon, I ask if she wants to do coffee, she says no. Another day, I try lunch again. She says no.

At the end of the week, I catch Ella by the lockers. "This weekend, want to watch a movie and order Chinese food?"

Not even looking at me, she says, "My family's got me super busy this weekend."

Ella's parents are often busy, but never with Ella.

I'm about to ask straight out what's going on when she suddenly looks up. "Why do you always ask me to eat?"

"What?"

"Do you think that's all I like to do?"

Startled, I say, "No, I just—"

Ella is actually glaring at me. I stammer, "I-it's what *I* like to do. I'm sorry, we can totally do something else."

She shakes her head. "Never mind."

"Ella, tell me what's going on, please."

"Nothing."

"Something happened at the dinner. . . ."

Her jaw tenses. A flicker of anger in her eyes. "Nothing new, believe me."

"Or maybe you're pissed at me. Tell me—what did I do?"

Frustrated, she slams the locker door. People around us jump.

"It's nothing you've done," she shouts, on the verge of tears. "It's me, okay?" She turns, starts hurrying away. "It's *me!*"

Helpless, I watch her go.

Then I hear behind me, "The tubby ones are always so temperamental. It's the imbalance of bodily energies."

I turn, see Cassandra. She's standing by the windows, the sun behind her. She's in darkness, but the immediate space around her is radiant, as if all her energy is shooting outward.

"What did you do to her, Cassandra? What did you say?"

"Nothing that wasn't true," she says innocently.

"This isn't funny; there's something not right with her."

"And I believe that's all that I said," she says, and walks past me.

I watch and wait, hoping Ella will crack and tell me what's going on. We say almost nothing on the walk to school now. Claiming she doesn't feel well, she brings her music and plugs it into her ears. Meanwhile, I walk beside her, praying she can at least hear my friendly thoughts.

And then one day, I walk out to the corner and Ella isn't there. No Scream bag. No bubble curls. No Ella.

I check my phone for a text. *Sorry, running late!* But there's no message.

I wait five minutes. Ten minutes. Then I text, *Hey there. Are you coming?*

As I stand there, I gaze at the three other corners that make up Eighty-Ninth and West End. One is empty and quiet. At another, a mom takes hold of her little girl's hand before they cross the street. A man checks his phone at a third.

I check my phone. No answer from Ella.

Maybe she's sick, I think, reluctantly starting to walk. Maybe she was up all night hurling and she's just too exhausted to get in touch. That happened to me once. It's not impossible.

But it's not what happened, and I know it.

All day, I keep checking my phone—even in class, which is an absolute no-no. In English, Mr. Rhinehart threatens to confiscate it if he sees it again. I like Mr. Rhinehart a lot. But I want to scream, *My friend could be in serious trouble, okay? Steinbeck can wait.*

A text from Nina about Peter Lilly picking his nose. One from my mom about dinner. Adam Zamora asking if we had to write three pages or five on the Federalist Papers. Nothing from Ella.

Then at the end of the day, I get a message from Cassandra. There are no words. Just a picture. It's an image from *Snow White,* the old Disney movie.

Snow White in her glass coffin.

CHAPTER SIXTEEN

I DITCH MY LAST CLASS AND head straight to Ella's building, a thousand hideous visions in my head. She lives just a few blocks up from me; I've been visiting her since fifth grade, so the doorman knows me. I slow down as I approach, in case he has something terrible to tell me. But he just touches his hat and waves me through. I hurry to the elevator, count silently as it climbs to the tenth floor.

Ella lives in one of those old Upper West Side buildings that has a maze of hallways leading to each apartment. I'm so desperate to get to her, I turn the wrong way and end up at the garbage chute. So I have to retrace my steps, start all over, make the right turn, before I find her apartment.

Probably I ring the buzzer way too long. When her mom answers the door, she looks annoyed. But annoyed is good, honestly. Way better than sobbing and hysteria.

Ms. Schaeffer is blocking the door. She doesn't have much to block it with: she's tiny. Like her sister, I think. Her brown-gray hair is frizzy, it brushes the shoulders of her jacket. Maybe it's my imagination, but I'm always a little intimidated by Ella's mom; I worry she thinks I'm some shallow, boy-crazy bimbo.

Now she says, "Hi, sweetie. Ella's asleep right now."

"Is she okay?"

Ms. Schaeffer looks surprised. "Oh, I think so. She woke up this morning and said she felt 'tired.' Between you and me, it seems like a case of 'I don't want to go to school–itis.'"

"So she'll be back tomorrow?"

"I would think so." She starts closing the door. "But I'll tell her you stopped by."

No, I think, I can't leave yet. No matter what her mother says, I know Ella's in trouble.

Stepping directly in her mom's line of vision, I say, "Happy birthday, by the way."

Startled, she lets go of the door. "Oh—thank you."

I fish. "Ella said it was quite a dinner."

"She did?" Ms. Schaeffer raises an eyebrow. "Was that what she was texting you?"

I make a guilty face. "Yeah, sorry about that."

"I told Ella—and I'll tell you too, Toni—I really don't like all this"—she waves her hands in the air, exactly like Ella does—"constant, meaningless chatter. Sometimes I think you girls don't even know what comes out of your mouths half the time. You just *bee, bee, bee, bee, bee.*" She makes high-pitched chipmunk noises. "In Ella's case, she's often talking about people she doesn't even know. I said to her at dinner, I can't imagine why you care about these things. Talk to your family, we are *right here.*"

I'm starting to get a picture of this dinner. "I'll really try and text less," I promise her.

"That would be nice," she says archly.

I turn to go, then have an idea. Looking back, I say, "Ms. Schaeffer?"

She was just about to close the door. Now she stops, irritated. "Hm?"

"I just want to say, I think what Cassandra said was wrong."

It's a total gamble. I don't know for a fact that Cassandra said anything. But from the look on Ms. Schaeffer's face, I know I'm on to something.

She says defensively, "I don't think she said anything untrue. We sent Ella to that clinic to learn ways to cope with stress other than eating. The night of my birthday, it was very clear she hadn't, and I think it was frustrating for everyone."

I imagine it: Ella surrounded by her family, scared of Cassandra. Once the phone was forbidden, food would have been her only distraction—her only defense. I can see her taking bite after bite after bite in that compulsive way she does when she's nervous.

Then Ms. Schaeffer says, "At any rate, her cousin simply asked Ella to tell her about her experience at the clinic."

Of course she did, I think.

"It was my sister who asked if the clinic had helped her understand the feelings behind her overeating. My brother-in-law suggested swimming as exercise. And her father and I said we were concerned for her. Now, I don't think that was terribly mean of us. But I suppose Ella feels we ganged up on her."

I have a memory of Chloe, Isabelle, and Zeena all crowding in on me that first day of school. I'll bet that's exactly what this dinner felt like to Ella. I had wondered how Cassandra could operate without allies. But she had her family. In one dinner, she took all the unhappiness and anxiety about Eamonn's death and turned it right on Ella. She made the family her coven.

She looks at me pointedly. "It would really help her, Toni, if her friends supported her in getting healthier."

"I will absolutely do that, Ms. Schaeffer. I promise."

Ella doesn't come to school the next day. She doesn't answer any of my texts. That afternoon, I sit on my bed and dial Ella's number. I am going to get through to her, I promise myself. No matter how many times I have to call.

The phone rings. No answer.

I call again.

No answer.

I call again.

No answer. I call again. Hear: "Hello?"

"Ella?"

"Oh. Hey."

Her voice is way slowed down. She sounds like she's half asleep. Or on some serious antianxiety meds.

"Did I wake you up?"

"Yeah. Sort of. I don't know. Not really . . ." She trails off.

"How are you?" I ask.

"I'm okay."

You really don't sound like it, I think.

"Your mom told me about the birthday dinner."

"Oh, that."

"Sounds like they were pretty mean to you."

"They were just . . . honest." A sickly laugh. "They did an intervention. Only I was the one who got all the truth thrown at her. Kind of trippy, huh?"

"Doesn't seem like it's helping you."

There's a pause. Then she says quietly, "Oh, it is. In a way."

"What are you doing now?"

"Uh, sleeping. I'm really tired."

I'm about to say, Yes, because you're seriously depressed and not eating, when Ella says, "Actually, I don't feel so much like talking."

Desperate, I say, "Ella?"

"I think I'm going to get off the phone. . . ."

"Can I come see you?"

"Take care," she whispers, and hangs up.

Snap out of it, Ella, I chant to myself in history the next day. Fight back. Break the spell. Cassandra is evil. Your family is nuts. Don't let them do this to you.

But day after day goes by and Ella does not come back to school.

One afternoon, I run into Cassandra outside the library. She makes a show of looking at the empty space next to me and says, "Hey, where's your bud? I hear she can't seem to get out of bed these days."

"How long does this last, Cassandra?"

She pretends to think about it. "Not sure. I left it kind of open-ended. I tried to take it easy, but Ella's so weak minded, I may have zapped her harder than I realized."

"Then maybe it's time to stop."

"Oh, I can't. The spell's been cast."

"Ella didn't mean to hurt you, you know that."

Cassandra rolls her eyes. "Yeah, news flash. Ninety-eight percent of the world's damage is caused by people who 'didn't mean to.'"

She walks away. Over her shoulder, she says, "You better get to work, sweetheart. You're letting me run away with this thing."

Between classes, I dial Ella's home line. Her mom picks up with "Yes?"

"Hi, Ms. Schaeffer, I'm so sorry. I wanted to know if you want me to pick up Ella's homework and bring it by. It's totally no problem."

A pause.

I add, "I mean, unless she's coming back soon . . ."

Ms. Schaeffer says, "I don't think you'll see Ella at school for a little while. She seems to be . . ."

"What?"

"Not herself," says Ms. Schaeffer. "But that would be good, if you could bring the work by. Thank you."

Ella's homeroom teacher is Ms. Megai. After school, I go to her classroom and get a folder full of homework. Not exactly a stress reducer for Ella, but it gives me an excuse to see her.

Then I go straight to Ella's building.

Ms. Schaeffer meets me at the door, says "Oh, thank you, Toni," and reaches for the folder.

But I hold it back. "Can I just see Ella for a little bit?"

She bites her lip. She doesn't look bored by Ella's situation anymore, she looks exhausted and worried. "I really don't know if it's a good idea, honey. She seems to get upset about the idea of visitors."

"I want to help."

"She's in a very fragile place right now, Toni. She's just sort of . . . shut down."

"I know. That's why I think she needs her friends," I plead. "She needs to know people care about her. Please? That's all I want to tell her."

She thinks. "Okay. But keep it calm, okay? Don't be surprised if she doesn't say much. She's not very chatty these days."

Depressed people usually aren't, I want to say.

When I crack the door, I see Ella lying in her bed, covered to the neck with blankets. The face that turns to me is pale and sweaty. The bouncy bubble hair is dark and damp on her skull. The eyes are huge, with no happiness in them. No nothing, actually. They're blank. The life seems like it's seeping out of her.

I step in, close the door. "Hey there, gorgeous girl."

She just stares at me.

"Can I sit down?" I want to give Ella any power I can, so she gets to choose. She looks at the chair near the bed to say yes.

There are three bedrooms in Ella's apartment; she has the smallest, because the second one is her parents' study. It feels even smaller because it's crammed with stuff. Ella doesn't throw anything away. Among her books, I see Frog and Toad and Judy

Blume alongside her Twilight books. Every stuffed animal she's ever owned has been kept. Plushy elephants and saggy rabbits crowd her armchair. In the corner, there's a big flat-screen. It's dark.

I take her hand. It's cold. "What's up with you, baby? I miss you."

I wait for her to answer. Instead, she looks out the window. "Ella?"

She still won't look at me.

"Sweetie, I know you're tired. You don't have to talk. Just . . . look at me, okay?"

Ella turns her head. But only to stare at the ceiling.

I decide to try another tactic. Making a stern face, I growl, "I'm serious here. I need Ella, and I want her back right now, missy."

Funny-bossy would have worked with Ella before. Not now. I don't have a clue as to how to get through to her. It's like there's a thick glass wall between us. I'm pounding on it, yelling. But Ella can't hear me.

I say, "Hey, want me to do a Shake Shack run? It's raspberry mix-in week."

Suddenly, Ella turns her head, fixes her eyes on me. At last, I have her attention.

She whispers, "She said you'd say that. That you'd try to get me to 'fall back into old patterns.'"

"Who?" I ask, although I know.

"Cassandra. That night at dinner, she said that you liked that I was fat, that it made you feel superior because you have this gorgeous body. Even my mom said you wouldn't help me change."

"Maybe I don't want you to change," I say. "Maybe I liked you the way you were."

Ella shakes her head, her hair sliding from side to side on the pillow.

"Come on, sweetie. This is Cassandra getting back at you for what you said. Don't let her freak you out."

She whispers, "It isn't just her. It's what they all think. They're all so"—the word comes out in a long, shuddering sigh—"disappointed. Especially my mom and dad."

"Oh, Ella," I say. "What your mom is, is worried."

"That's just another word for disappointed. That whole time"—Ella's eyes are still on the ceiling, but she's struggling to speak—"that they were yelling at me about the phone and the way I eat, I thought, Oh, you thought Cassandra needed the help, but they don't see it that way. To them, you're the crazy one. You're the one who needs to change."

She glances at me. "I looked at Cassandra when it was going on. She knew. She was smiling. All the times our moms compared us—she was like, Yeah, you see now, I won. You are officially the family mess."

She looks back at the ceiling. "After that, all the energy just went right out of me. I sat there thinking, Don't eat another bite or they'll freak. And you better not say anything, 'cause . . . everything you say is stupid. And that's when it kind of came to me."

"What did?"

"Don't talk. Don't eat. Just keep your mouth shut. Then they can't . . ."

She trails off. "Then they can't what, Ella?"

"Get me."

I squeeze her hand hard, wanting to say, But she *has* gotten you, Ella.

Her eyelids flutter. "Maybe, if I do what they want, they won't be so mad at me."

My eyes sting with tears. "But you can't stay like this forever."

Ella shakes her head slightly. "Nothing else to do."

"Please, don't go away." I squeeze her hand again. "Please?"

Her eyes widen slightly; I know she's listening, even if she doesn't want to.

But then she looks hard at the gray sky beyond her window and her expression becomes empty. The glass wall is back and there is only silence.

As I walk home, I think and think about how to help Ella. If I go to her parents, what would I say? I could tell them about Cassandra. But I can imagine them saying, Spells? What do you mean? How could Cassandra be hurting our daughter?

What is a spell? I wonder. And how do you break it? I remember the feeling that I was pounding on glass, trying to make Ella hear me. So, how do you break that damn glass?

All of a sudden, I remember that picture Cassandra sent me. Taking out my phone, I look at it. Snow White in her glass coffin. Not dead—but unreachable.

At first, I took it as a declaration of war. Now I'm wondering. Maybe it's a clue.

When I get back, I tell my parents I'm not hungry and go straight to my room. In a box under my bed are all my old tapes and DVDs. Kneeling on the floor, I pull the box out and cough from all the dust. I grab Snow White, examine the cover. There she is, surrounded by weeping dwarves, with the prince arriving on horseback.

The witch puts her to sleep, I think. Coma, really. A state of nonbeing where no one can reach her. And there's always something these princesses do to themselves that causes it: Snow White eats the apple. Sleeping Beauty pricks herself with a spindle. The hate that Cassandra has for her, her parents' disappointment—Ella's taken it all in. She's eaten the apple, swallowed the poison, made it part of herself.

So, the witch can't do it completely on her own. But once it's done, it's done. The princess can't save herself.

Which kind of sucks. What the hell, Brothers Grimm?

Someone has to save the princess. Usually that someone is a prince. But Ella has no prince that I know of. Unless you count Liam Hemsworth, who she has a huge crush on. But I doubt he's going to be willing to come to New York and lay one on a teenage girl to bring her back to life.

Also—if Oliver taught me anything, it's don't wait for the cute guy on horseback.

But maybe it doesn't have to be a prince. Or maybe . . . I can be the prince. So how does the prince bring the princess back to life?

He kisses her, of course. But I don't think me kissing Ella is going to do much.

Why a kiss? What does the kiss tell you?

I guess that someone loves you. That you're not alone. So where do I find this magic kiss?

I look at the postcards on my wall. I stare at my idols, Bette Davis and Dorothy Parker, wondering what they'd do. All I can think is, They wore such intense, dark lipstick in those days.

And then I have an idea.

* * *

The very next day, I cut lunch and go to a stationery store. I buy ten pieces of colored oak tag and some markers. Then I stop at a drugstore and buy five cheap lipsticks.

When I come back, I'm storing the stuff in my locker when Abby Cronin comes up to me. "Hey, how's Ella?"

Is Abby deigning to speak to me? She must see the surprise on my face, because she says, "Ella and I have English together. Is it true she had some kind of breakdown?"

What *would* you call what Cassandra has done to Ella? I guess "nervous breakdown" works. "Yeah, she's not well. Feeling really, really down on herself right now."

"That's not right," says Abby sadly.

I've never seen Abby actually concerned about someone. Usually she's just . . . angry.

Saying "I agree," I pull out one of the poster boards and hold up a lipstick. "Want to help me help her?"

I explain to Abby what I want her to do and why. At first she says, "That's a little weird. Can I just write something?"

"Nope," I say, and hand her the lipstick. "Everybody gives Ella a kiss, that's the rule. I want this girl to feel seriously loved."

Abby laughs. "Okay."

She smears the lipstick on her mouth and gives the poster board a big *mwah*.

Then she writes: "Dear Ella, you're a good soul. Please get well soon."

Handing it back, she says, "Oh, wait a minute." She takes it back, scribbles her number. "Tell her to call me sometime."

"I will," I say, thinking, One down, hundreds to go. Many of whom are not so crazy about me. Still, I have to try. My individual energy isn't strong enough to save Ella. I need a coven.

In the library, I slide the card to Nina Watts, who says, "What's this?" She sees Abby's note. "Oh, Fudgie the Whale."

She smiles, expecting me to get the joke. Because, hey, she doesn't hate Ella, she's just having a laugh.

When I don't respond, she says, "Come on, she'd say it herself."

"That kind of joke is part of what's making her sick." I hold up the lipstick. "You're a cool person, Nina. Help me out."

Nina considers, then reaches for the lipstick. "Free makeup? Who am I to say no?"

She writes: "Yo, El. Get your butt back here. I miss your goofy ass."

Just then I feel a tap on the shoulder. I turn, see Amber Davies. Amber's this elfin little creature with a dark-brown bob and killer dimples. She runs with the art crowd. She says, "Is that a get-well card for Ella?"

"Yeah." I show her. "Kind of a kiss-and-tell."

"Can I sign it?" I hand her the card, pen, and lipstick. As she writes, Amber says, "She was super sweet to me when I got suspended."

That's right, I think. Everyone died laughing when Amber got caught coming to school stoned on her parents' supply. But Ella stuck up for her.

Amber says, "I was feeling totally horrible, but she was like, Aw, man, you get to catch up on the soaps. Which I don't even watch, but making a joke made it all seem less dire, you know?"

She writes, "For Ella, a way fabulous chick. Miss you!" Then she draws a little image of Ella with her bubble curls and her Scream bag. Giving the board a big kiss, she says, "I really hope she feels better."

Amber gives me an idea for my next target: Paul Jarrett, who dealt with a lot of comments after kissing David Horvath. I don't know Paul that well, and I don't know if he knows Ella said nice things about him when that happened. But it's worth a shot.

I track him down in the gym, shooting hoops after school. As the ball clangs against the backboard, I hold up the card and call out, "Hi. I'm doing a get-well card for Ella Schaeffer?"

He holds the ball close, says carefully, "Okay."

"Yeah. She's struggling right now, and she's the kind of person who always says nice things about people?" I get no recognition from Paul's expression. "So I'm thinking we could support her in return."

Paul says quickly, "Yeah—cool."

He hesitates over the lipstick, but does it quickly, then goes back to his jump shot.

I read what he's written: "Ella—don't let 'em get you down."

The school day is over. I've gotten everyone I'm going to get today. I head back down to my locker to get my stuff. On the stairs, I hear, "Hey, can I sign?"

I turn, see Cassandra. She's standing a few steps above me. I call up, "This is for people who wish Ella well."

"Oh." Cassandra looks sad. "Yeah, not really me, then."

She walks down the steps until she reaches me. "Small piece of advice?"

"Very small."

"The kids here are weak. Easily distracted. Not great material for a coven."

"You might be surprised," I tell her.

In the story of *Sleeping Beauty,* the prince has to fight his way through the forest of thorns to save the princess. If he can do that, I tell myself, I can survive the cafeteria at lunchtime.

It's been a while since I've been here on my own. Slam the Slut is no longer everyone's favorite game, but you never know what could happen. Holding the poster in front of me like a shield, I search out friendly faces. I see Wallace, who's a fellow reality-TV junkie, and Reina Goldfarb, who's Ella's homeroom bestie. Both of them sign the card. But there's still a whole lot of space left.

But as Reina puts the cap back on the lipstick, Lizbeth Dawson turns from the table where she's sitting with her rugby buds. "Hey, what's this?"

"Um, for Ella?" I tell her. "She's kind of . . ."

"Having a breakdown," offers Reina cheerfully. "So we're sending love."

Lizbeth says, "Oh, man, I'm sorry. She's a sweetie. Here"—she holds her hand out for the card—"we'll sign."

After the entire rugby team has signed, Lizbeth stands up on the bench and shouts, "Kisses for Ella, y'all. One of our own needs help, let's do it!"

Suddenly, everybody wants to sign Ella's card. People egg each other on to do big smacks and nice messages. When the card is held up for the next person, people wave their hands, frantic to be chosen. Some of the guys balk at the lipstick, but it quickly becomes uncool to refuse. All over the room, you hear laughter as kids tell stories about Ella. Some of them are a little teasing, but they're all affectionate.

Finally, the card makes its way back to Lizbeth, who gives it back to me. Holding up the card, I call out, "Thanks so much, everybody! I'm going to take these to Ella and—"

Just then Zeena, Isabelle, and Jackson Kinroth enter the cafeteria. The room starts to buzz—no words you can hear, but you sure feel it. Chloe's friends are here. *She's* here.

At the sight of me, Zeena narrows her eyes. Isabelle looks panicked. Jackson grins, his hand going to the edge of his shirt. But he stops; Zeena might not appreciate him leering at me in front of her. He looks around. *What's the joke? What's the gag? What do we have for her today?*

His eyes fall on Wallace Laird, who's trying to fade into the Formica. Jackson grins, calls out, "Hey, Laird. Why don't you sit over here? Even you could score with this chick."

Wallace is confident when he's with normal people who know he's gay and are cool with it, but like most of us, he's not as tough when someone treats him like garbage. He has no defenses against a pure idiot like Jackson. He flushes bright red, tries to pretend he didn't hear.

I scramble for something sharp and witty to say, something that will take the power away from Jackson and Zeena. Then Isabelle coughs.

In a very small voice, but loud enough to be heard, she says to Jackson, "You're seriously . . . gross."

Then she wobbles over and stands next to me. She looks like she's going to burst into tears out of nerves—but she's here.

I say, "Jackson, Wallace over you any day of the week and twice on Sundays." And Wallace says, "Thanks, but if I have a choice, I'm going for Jeremy Renner." I pretend to be furious and throw a napkin in his direction.

There's a ripple of laughter. It grows. And in the laughter, a warmth, a happiness, even. I think of that old song, *War is over if you want it*. I do want it. There may never be a day when I don't think of Chloe, what she did to me and what I did to her. But I want no more war.

"Hi," I say to Isabelle.

"Hi," she says back.

I hold up the card. "Want to sign?"

In my history class, I get Malaya Chen and Bill "Pigman" Pullman. The next morning, I get everyone in my homeroom—and in Ella's. Her homeroom teacher, Ms. Megai, raises an eyebrow at the lipstick. "Everyone using one lipstick? A bit unsanitary, isn't it?"

But she signs, saying, "I hope Ella comes back soon. Tell her it's not the same without her."

The people who work in the lunchroom all sign. Her whole Spanish class writes, *"Te queremos, Ella! Enviamos besos!"*

By the end of the day, I have 153 besos.

One hundred fifty-three kisses to bring Ella back to life.

CHAPTER SEVENTEEN

THAT AFTERNOON, I BRING FIVE posters to Ella's house. First I show them to her mom when she opens the door. Reading what people wrote, she starts to tear up, then attacks her eyes with fists, wiping the tears away.

"Ella's got a lot of fans," I say.

Her mom inhales, like she's trying to breathe in all the goodwill. Then she waves a hand down the hall. "Go, take them to her."

Ella looks surprised as I come in; surprise is good, I think. Surprise is interest. I'll take it.

"Hey," I tell her. "I brought something for you."

I set the posters up on her desk, so she can see how many signatures I got. "From everyone at school."

"Get-well cards," she says flatly.

"No," I say. "Not exactly. These are kisses, Ella. One from Pigman Pullman, even. You can't call that your everyday get-well card. I mean, maybe gross. Maybe cootie-ridden . . ."

Ella looks away.

I bring the first card to her bed. "At least read the messages," I tell her.

She sighs. "'Dear Ella, get well soon. Love so-and-so.'"

"But look at the so-and-so's." I point to Paul Jarrett's message, then to Amber's. Ella smiles a little when she sees Amber's note.

I point to Abby's message. "From Abby, who would like you to call her."

Ella reads the good-soul message. Frowns thoughtfully.

"And here's from your homeroom teacher." I point to the lip print.

Ella's eyes widen. She whispers, "You got *her* to wear lipstick?"

"I did," I say, thrilled with her reaction. "She worried about germs and said the color was a 'tad bold' for her, but for you, she'd risk it."

I get the rest of the cards and spread them on her bed like a blanket. Ella gazes at the messages, lightly touches the kiss marks. "Come back soon, honey! I miss your beautiful smile," from Linda in the lunchroom. "*Te amo,* Ella!" from Carl Whittaker in her Spanish class. And "I've been there, it hurts. Let's do yogurt!" from Isabelle.

Lizbeth wrote, "Stay strong. Ever thought of playing rugby?"

Ella croaks, "Yeah, right." But she's smiling.

She keeps reading, and as she does, she comments more and more. "Oh, sweet," and "God, I didn't know he knew I existed," and "I thought she hated me." The more she talks, the more the cobwebs in her voice clear.

"You know," I say, "I didn't run across a single person who doesn't like you."

Ella glances toward the door. Then she pushes the cards away. "You didn't look in the right place, then."

She's talking about her family. At first I don't know what to say. Ella's parents love her, but they are too harsh on her.

I say, "Ella, your family might not like the way you eat or the so-called silly things you talk about—"

She looks at me, curious.

"But I don't care how you eat and I *do* like the things you talk about. And so do a lot of other people."

"I talk too much about other people," she says sadly.

"Maybe. But maybe that's because you never felt like you were interesting enough to talk about."

She smiles a little. "Well, let's be real—I'm not."

"And here's another thing," I tell her. "Why did Amber and Paul sign those cards? Because when you talked about them, you stuck up for them. You always stick up for people who are getting slammed. Like when you defended me to Ramona Digby."

She shakes her head. "I should've done more for you. I feel so bad about that."

"You stayed my friend," I say. "You cared what happened to me. You tried to stop me from getting stomped by Chloe— remember, you offered to walk me home?"

She nods.

"So don't say you didn't do anything."

She pulls one of the cards closer. Then says, "I shouldn't have said what I did about Cassandra and Eamonn."

"I disagree." Startled, she looks up. "Your whole family was tied up in knots. Everyone was wondering, nobody was saying anything because"—I swallow—"because it's really horrible to think about and who could handle any more pain? But it needed to be said, Ella."

"I didn't say it because I was so noble," she says. "At the time, I thought, 'Look how great I am, revealing the big ugly truth.' But really, I just wanted my family to hate Cassandra instead of me."

I think about this. "It can be both, can't it? I still think it was a good thing, even if it came from a stinky place."

Ella's mouth jerks in an almost smile at the word "stinky." Then she catches sight of herself in the mirror over her bureau. She says, "'Mirror, mirror on the wall—who's the grossest one of all?'"

"Yeah—time to break that mirror. That one belongs to your family. What does yours show?"

"Oh, that's a really ugly sight."

"Then let's change it."

Ella pushes the cards around with the tip of her finger. "How?"

"Why don't you try to be as nice to yourself as you are to other people?"

She rolls her eyes. "I'm not *that* nice."

I point to the cards. "I think all those guys would seriously disagree."

Ella touches Amber's and Abby's notes.

"But there is one thing you have to do for yourself," I tell her.

"Like what?"

"Like get out of that bed."

Her eyebrows shoot up. "Whoa. Seriously?"

"So seriously."

Ella pretends to consider it. Then carefully she sets the posters aside. Pushes back the covers. Her creased nightgown is tangled around her knees. Her legs and feet are pale and stubbly on the wrinkled sheets.

"It feels so hard," she whispers. "I know that's pathetic, but it feels really, really hard."

"I'm here for you, Ella," I tell her. "So are a lot of people."

She puts her hands flat on the mattress, pushes herself up. "Oog . . ."

"Stiff, huh?"

"Just a little." She swings one leg so the foot dangles over the edge. She peers down at the floor. "Remember that game where you'd pretend a part of the floor was the ocean and it was full of sharks? If you touched it, they'd chomp off your toes?"

"Mine was lava pits, but I get you."

Ella touches her toes to the floor, pulls her foot back up onto the mattress. "I am actually kind of scared," she says.

"I know."

She looks at me. Then down at the ground. Lurching sideways, she rolls off the bed, landing not on her feet, but on her ass.

I freeze, terrified Ella will take this as a sign.

But instead she cracks up laughing.

Clapping a hand to her forehead, she gasps, "Oh, my God! Oh my God. I am such a crazy person."

Laughing, I plop down beside her and I hug her hard. "Ella, you're the freaking best."

She looks around. "Did I break my leg?"

"I don't think so."

"Oh? Oh, well then. Here goes." She puts a hand on the side of her bed, lifts herself up. When she's upright, she plants her hand on her hip and says, "Here she is, boys! Here she is, world! Here's . . ."

"Ella!" we scream.

An hour later, I pass by the living room, where Ella's mom is on the phone. I hear, "Well, the therapist said—"

Someone interrupts, and she interrupts them back, saying, "I know, Martin, she—"

Then she sees me, widens her eyes, makes a gesture that she wants to talk to me. But I can see she and Mr. Schaeffer are having an argument. So I mouth, "I'll be back," and she goes back to talking to Ella's dad.

Walking home, I think of Ella's parents. I wish they had clued in to Ella's feelings before all this happened. But then, I wish I had too.

I think of what's waiting at my house. My mom is going out with friends—again. This is the fourth friends night in two weeks. For my mother who used to say her idea of heaven was eating while she read a book and didn't have to talk to anyone. In fact, that was one of the things that brought my parents together. My dad saw my mom reading a book in a noisy bar all by herself and thought, Yeah, that's my kind of lady.

But this hypersocialness doesn't feel good. I wonder if my mom is showing my dad she can leave the family too. Or is she . . . like, actually planning to leave? So many bummer questions, so few answers.

When I get home, my dad will be there. I can suggest we order Thai food—"Pad Thai! Larb, extra spicy"—to put happiness in this house where there is none. But I feel tired at the thought of it.

Really, it's simple. My mom is not in the house because Katherine still is. You can feel her everywhere, in the silences, the things we don't do, the boring conversations that fall apart like stale crackers. You feel her in my mom's anger, my dad's guilt. My mom can't stop being angry. She's trying, I know, but it's not working. She can't get back to us.

And slowly, my dad is getting tired of feeling guilty. He's getting tired of trying. My mom's anger is like a death grip on his throat, choking the life out of him. After a while, he'll stop fighting.

And then what happens? When everyone decides it's just not worth it?

I'm not sure. But I'm starting to realize there's no magic spell I can work.

Of course, it's not just the kisses that bring Ella back to life. She has to form her own coven, with Shelley, her therapist, with her parents, who go with her to therapy sometimes, and with her friends. I visit Ella every day. Sometimes Reina comes. Once Amber came with me, another time Abby. Amber is hilariously dippy in the same way Ella is; at times, I worry I could be replaced as bestie-in-chief. But now is not the time for jealousy. Different friends can do different things for you.

I also worry about Abby because she's so bossy. But she is fiercely loyal, and Ella can use that kind of support. Every time she puts herself down, Abby is right there with a comeback.

In the elevator as we leave Ella's apartment, Abby is quiet. Then she says thoughtfully, "I was a judgmental dingus to you at the beginning of the year."

I laugh. Hyperarticulate Abby using the word "dingus." Also, hyper-righteous Abby apologizing.

I say, "Mistakes were made by all."

"Yeah," she agrees as we walk out onto the street. "But not by me. I'm perfect."

Her face is totally deadpan. And when I laugh, she does too.

I walk Abby home, then head for my place. It's dark early now. Remembering the week, the cards, everyone who visited, I can't help but think, All this is great. But it's not enough.

For the spell to be broken, truly broken, the witch has to die.

Two days later, Ella calls me. "So, next week?"

"Yeah?"

"I might be coming back to school. The therapist says she thinks I'm ready."

"Welcome back, beauty."

The following Monday morning when I meet Ella on the corner, I hand her a small box. "Ooh," she says, her eyes sparkling. "Presents. Can I open it now?"

"Sure."

Her fingers work the ribbon and tissue paper. Inside is a small box. Inside the box is Gloriana the butterfly.

"Oh, my God," she breathes. "One of your little creatures. She's so beautiful, I love this one." She takes Gloriana out of the box, holds her up to the light. "You sure you want to give her up? You have a whole set."

Had, I think, remembering destroyed Phoebe. "They don't need to huddle all together anymore," I say lightly. "I think they're ready to move on." I touch Gloriana's wing. "She belongs with you because she's gorgeous and lighthearted and she makes people happy. Look at her when you forget about yourself."

Ella hugs me. "Thank you. I will take such good care of her."

We start to walk. Ella tells me about her recent shrink session with her parents. "My mom keeps saying how terrible she feels. It takes like, half the session. Meanwhile my dad's like, 'I'm happy you're better.'" She drops her voice low to imitate her dad. "'Now let's think nutritionist.' Then Shelley asked me what I thought about that. I said, 'Well, I agree about the nutritionist. But I kind of wish food wasn't the first thing my dad thinks of when he thinks of me.' I was totally terrified my dad would lose it. But Shelley said, 'Did you hear that, Martin?' Which is shrinkese for 'Score!'"

I grin. "Fab-o-rama."

She nods happily, then goes quiet for a little while. Just before we get to school, she says suddenly, "I went to see Cassandra this weekend."

Amazed, I say, "Why?"

"Because I wanted to apologize for starting this whole Eamonn thing. Maybe in a way, it was good to clear the air? But I did it to get back at her too, and that really rots."

"Yeah, but they *need* to be in therapy, Ella."

"Well, that's the thing. They still haven't gone. Her parents keep making dates and Cassandra refuses to show up. So I wanted to tell her family therapy's not that bad."

"What happened?" I ask.

"Her parents were out at a movie with my parents, so I knew she'd be alone. First thing she said was 'Oh, back from the dead.' Which was a little weird, but whatever. I said, 'Look, I'm here because I owe you an apology.'"

"What'd she say?"

"Oh, she rolled her eyes, like Give me a break. And I said, No, really. I screwed up and I want you to know that I know that. Then I told her how I thought our parents had always compared us and made us compete and how we should really be friends. Because who else understands how crazy our family can be?"

"And?"

"She says to me, 'You don't even have the first clue what you're apologizing for.' I said, 'Well, as a matter of fact, I do know. I am sorry for talking about Eamonn and I am sorry that I said in any way that you hurt him or let him die or whatever. That was sucky and wrong and I really, really apologize.'"

The light turns red. Ella and I are stuck at the corner. I press, "So what did Cassandra say?"

"Well, this is where it really gets insane. *She* said, 'Oh, that's what you told people, huh? That I killed Eamonn?' Her voice was all calm, no big deal. I said, Yes, unfortunately, I kind of did, and I understand if you hate my guts and never speak to me again."

"Then?"

Ella takes a deep breath. "Then she said, 'But I did kill Eamonn.'"

We're almost at the school. Neither of us knows what to say.

Luckily, behind us, Reina Goldfarb shrieks, "Oh, my God, yay, Ella!"

That's all it takes for Ella to be swarmed by kids. Everyone hugging, patting, exclaiming. It's a flash mob of Ella love. Somehow we all stumble into the building. Ella and I get separated on the stairs as she's practically carried off to her locker. She grins back at me. I wave, call, "See you at lunch!" She gives me a thumbs-up before she disappears through the second-floor doors.

I have a huge, dumb smile on my face. And for a while, I just stand there with that smile. Feeling good.

Then I think of Cassandra. Who told Ella she killed Eamonn.

Is that why she won't go to therapy?

I imagine it. Cassandra on one side of the office, sunk deep in a chair, chin fixed on her fist, looking away as her parents try to reach her, the therapist tries to reach her.

They won't reach her. She won't let them.

But someone has to. Whether she did do what she said or she didn't . . . someone has to help her.

I should really leave it alone.

Only . . .

Cassandra didn't leave me alone. Maybe I would have been better off if she had. But even with all that's gone down between us, I still remember that when I was on the bathroom floor, a mess of piss and tears and pain, Cassandra was the one who got me on my feet.

By now, I should get that there is no magic between me and Cassandra. That we can't read each other's minds. That if I want to talk to her, I have to pick up the phone.

And yet I do feel like we have a connection. And that's a kind of magic.

Yo, Cassandra.

I wait.

Then hear *Go away.*

I feel it anyway. She's in a bad, hurting place.

Come on, babe. Talk to me.

GO AWAY!

Where are you, Cassandra?

No answer.

Where would you be? I wonder.

And then I know.

CHAPTER EIGHTEEN

SHE'S SITTING AT THE VERY end of the rock, the part I used to think of as the whale's head. Her back is to me, she sits huddled in her coat, waiting for something. I imagine the whale's body smashing back down into the water after breaching, that enormous weight pulling everything down with it.

Without turning, Cassandra says, "So you brought her back to life."

"Not just me. There were a lot of kisses on those cards."

"Was it worth it?"

Such a weird question. So Cassandra. As I think of what to say, I find myself not thinking about Ella—but about Chloe. I remember Oliver running away from me on the street. The ragged hole Chloe's death left in his life. Chloe's little sister crying at the funeral. How I'll never get to see Chloe at class reunions and think, Oh, you changed, you're an okay person now. Or, Still the same old bitch, big surprise. And how much I would give, here and now, to have the chance to find out which it was.

"Yeah, it was worth it," I say.

"Funny," says Cassandra. "I usually feel when people are gone, that's when you realize what a major pain in the ass they were. You're not supposed to say that, of course. You have to do the whole 'Oh, how can we go on without them'? deal. When really—you're relieved."

"You don't really feel relieved that Eamonn died," I tell her.

"Yes, I do," she says numbly. "That's why I killed him."

Images in the head, the ones I haven't fully allowed to form. Cassandra shoving Eamonn under the water, holding him down, getting soaked as he thrashes, but waiting, waiting . . .

Until everything is quiet.

"Tell me what happened, Cassandra."

Still sitting, she spins around to face me. "Have you ever known someone like Eamonn? Spent any kind of time with them?"

"No." I sit down on the rock, the whale's neck.

"It—" Cassandra breaks off, stares out at the river. This time, words are not coming easily to her. "I don't know, maybe you think all autistic people are like . . . Spock or something. They don't feel things, they don't get emotion. Like they're dateless geeks at school, but they win the Nobel Prize for Physics and it all kind of works out okay."

"The guys on *Big Bang Theory.*"

"Right. Well, that wasn't Eamonn. Eamonn didn't have an outside skin. All his nerve endings were right there on the surface. The stuff you and I deal with without even thinking could cause a total neural meltdown for Eamonn. The wrong kind of shirt. The wrong kind of light, voice a little too loud. Once my aunt picked up one of his trains, put it down in the wrong place. He had them all lined up, you see, just the way they should be. Eamonn flipped. She was like, What's wrong with him? I was like, How would you like it if someone came stomping into your world and messed it all up?"

I think of Katherine. "Not a whole lot."

"Damn right. And when Eamonn didn't like something, he screamed. As if he was on fire. And it could go on for hours. No joke."

"So you were careful," I say.

"Yep. Keep the energy around Eamonn calm and quiet. Don't talk too loud. Nothing on TV with loud bangs. No fighting, obviously. You couldn't drop a pot, slam a door, or—"

Have any feelings whatsoever, I think.

Cassandra says, "I could calm him down. I was good at it. Either I got less freaked than my parents or—"

"You had the special powers."

She nods approvingly. "I would warm up his favorite blanket, wrap him tight, and hold his head to mine. Forehead to forehead." She smiles. "Then I'd sing 'Yellow Submarine.' Usually that got him calm enough that we could get him into a warm—"

She breaks off, and I realize the next word would have been "bath."

"Nice spell casting," I say.

"Not shabby."

"So what happened that night?"

I feel Cassandra pull into herself, go dark.

"What did you mean when you said your parents left you guys alone one too many times?"

"What does it sound like?" she says bitterly.

"Did you usually babysit for him?"

"Who else were they going to get? We spent so much on his therapies and his school and his this and his that, we couldn't afford a babysitter. The few we did try had no clue how to handle him."

"So make Cassandra do it."

She looks at me. "I wanted to. I loved Eamonn."

"I know. I've never, ever not known that." I pause. "What happened?"

"I told you. I willed him to die." She sings, "'I put a spell on you—because you're mi-ine. Yes, you're mine.'"

"You didn't do that, Cassandra." More and more, I feel sure of this.

"Oh, but I did. You of all people know we can cause people to die. Everyone wants to pretend people don't have that power, to kill with our feelings. But we do. And we do it all the time. You just have to find the weak spot and press."

She smiles a horrible smile. I say, "Chloe died in a terrible, horrible accident, Cassandra. People get hit by cars all the time. It's not witchcraft."

"Really? Did she get hit or did she just walk on out into the street because her world was falling apart and she didn't want to live anymore?" When I don't answer, she wonders out loud, "And who made her not want to live anymore? Who made her feel that the man she loved was going to leave her?"

I want to snap, Chloe drank too much and walked in front of a truck. End of story.

Only I don't. Because I remember Isabelle saying, *She was convinced you were out to get her. She kept saying she "felt" you thinking about her. Said she could practically hear you.*

That's what Chloe *felt*, not fact.

Except I *was* out to get her.

Chloe was insecure and unhappy before anything happened with me and Oliver. She was taking her fear out on other people and the school threatened to suspend her. And yeah, she got drunk that night, and yeah, her friends should have looked out for her better. Chloe died for a million things that had nothing to do with me.

But I was another one of those things. And I didn't have to be. And I have to live with that and remember that. Cassandra's right. We do have power to hurt and sometimes kill with our feelings. And if you don't understand that, you could end up doing a lot of damage.

Find the weak spot and press. That's what Cassandra's doing to me right now, trying to distract me by playing on my guilt about Chloe. I have to stay focused.

I say again, "What happened that night, Cassandra?"

She opens her mouth and I can see from her expression, she's going to be flip. But then she stops. When she speaks again her voice is soft, as if it's coming from far away.

"It wasn't the greatest week. Eamonn was probably coming down with a cold and it made him really cranky. My parents had a work thing to go to. Normally, they don't both go to those things, but . . ."

"But."

She takes a deep breath. "My dad was like, We need to get out of the house. And I said, Yeah, go. Because I could see they were on the verge of losing it. Eamonn had been . . . tough that week." Her eyes darken and I can see it hurts to admit that.

"What about you?"

"What about me?"

"Were you on the verge, like your mom and dad?"

"I'm stronger than they are," she says simply. "They're the parents. There's a lot of emotion for them, a lot of guilt. Not to mention it hurt their pride to have a kid who wasn't, in their eyes, a high achiever. Ella may have mentioned that's a thing with our family."

"Okay."

"Okay," she echoes, returning to the story. "So, like I said, Eamonn had a cold, everyone was wrecked, my parents went out—only Eamonn didn't want them to go."

"Why not?"

She shrugs. "Who knows? Just kept screaming, 'Not Cassandra, I don't want Cassandra!' Hanging on to them, flapping, hitting, the whole lovely deal. And my mom's looking at me suspiciously, like, Why doesn't he want you, why aren't you making this stop?"

"*Maybe* you're imagining that?"

"Oh, no," she says cheerfully. "At one point, she snapped, 'Cassie, just *do* something.' So I took Eamonn by both arms and pulled. Really, really hard. Not recommended in the autism handbook, by the way. I looked at my parents and thought, You want him out of your hair? Fine, he's gone. Have a nice time."

"Then what?"

"Then they left."

"And what did Eamonn do?"

"Oh, he had a complete meltdown. Screamed. Kicked. Pulled his hair. Bit his arms. Pulled my hair. Bit my arms. It was really fun. I did the blanket thing, tried to hold his head, sang 'Yellow Submarine.' And it was almost starting to work—I think? When this jerk from downstairs started banging on the door and yelling, 'You shut that kid up! He should be in an institution!' And I totally lost it and screamed, 'Really? You should be euthanized.'"

"And after that?"

"Uh, after that, I kind of felt like my head was going to explode. Like, yay me, defending Eamonn, but the yelling really did not improve the situation. He was worse than before."

She looks at me for a long time, as if leaving it up to me to end the conversation. When I don't, she continues in an odd, detached voice. "Normally when Eamonn freaks, I get very, very calm. Like he takes all my crazy energy and burns it for me so I can be totally Zen. But that was not working this time. His energy was, ah, really getting into my head. He just kept thrashing around and yelling, 'No, no, not you! Not you!' I tried to give him some meds, he threw them across the floor. And I'm trying to get my hands on more and freaking out about the guy downstairs. Plus being scared for Eamonn, *and* mad at him for scaring me."

"What'd you do?"

"Here's where I got really brilliant. I came up with this crazed notion that I could out-scream him. You know in those absurd Harry Potter movies, when people hurl energy at each other? That's what I was thinking. Like, Oh, you're slamming me with your rage? I'm gonna slam you with mine, and we'll see who's bigger, huh?"

"And then?"

"I yelled at him, 'Oh, give me a break, Eamonn, you're just doing this because you can. Must be nice to have everyone under your spell, totally in your power all the time.'"

Cassandra's voice breaks. There's so much pain in her eyes as she remembers her words. "You'd had enough," I tell her.

"Yeah, that's a really good excuse," she says in a low voice. "Right up there with 'I didn't mean to.'"

She's quiet a moment, then says, "He was crying so much, I started hitting myself. So I wouldn't hit him. That's when I realized, This is crazy, this is awful and it's all going to get so . . . much . . . worse."

Now the tears are running down her face, but she doesn't bother with them.

"So I was like, Honey, honey, we need to get you into a bath. But he . . . he was still gonzo and it was really hard to get him in the bathroom and I was trying to fill up the tub and get him undressed and keep him from slamming his head against the sink. And the screaming was really piercing my brain and I—"

The horror of it jams up her throat; I can feel it, a ball of sharp, tangled wire cutting her inside. In a shred of voice, she says, "And I just pushed him into the tub and I yelled, 'Now stay there! You stay there!' And I went to my room and I put on my headphones because I needed not to hear him for just a little while and—"

She sobs. "And I didn't hear him. He must have seized in the bathtub, and I didn't hear the thrashing or the water or anything. I didn't hear him and he died, and I made him die, I did, I . . . killed him and . . ."

I scramble to my feet, wrap her up in my arms. "You didn't mean for him to die—"

She shoves me away, hard. "Stop it! Do not—" She strangles on the rage. "Do not tell me I didn't mean for that to happen. I *knew.* I knew better. I had power and Eamonn had no power and I used my power and he died."

Yes, I think helplessly, a lot of that is true. But it is also true that Cassandra loved Eamonn and she'd had no idea that he would die. Why won't she see that?

Then I realize it's better to decide that you have powers that you can control than admit you got overwhelmed and freaked out and a horrible, horrible thing happened. Better evil power than no power at all.

Cassandra has moved to the edge of the whale's head. The broad slope starts off smooth and straight. At the bottom, the rocks break up, become jagged. She's turned away from me. I have to get her back.

I move to sit behind her, giving her just enough room.

I say softly, "Can I tell you a story?"

"What kind of story?"

"A fairy tale. Sort of."

In a raw voice, Cassandra says, "Oh, come on." But she doesn't move.

"Once upon a time, a baby girl was born. Let's say she was a princess. And this princess grew up to be a good, strong, smart person. So strong and so smart that she took care of everyone around her. One day, her mother and father brought a new baby home. A little boy. But the prince was not like his sister. He had power, but a very different power. He frightened people—even his parents—with his terrible rage. Only his sister the princess knew how to calm him. And she did, because she was a good person and she loved him."

Cassandra turns back to me.

"But she didn't have a lot of help, and little by little, she got tired. Then one day, a handsome young man, a beautiful, dark-eyed lad, came to her village and said, 'Hey, gorgeous. You want to have some fun?'"

"And what did she say?" Cassandra asks.

"She said, Hell yes. And off with him she went. Only a few weeks later, he vanished. Because he wasn't strong and he wasn't that smart or brave and he didn't want to take care of anybody. So the princess was left on her own again."

"Then what?"

"She went home. Back to her mother and father. Back to her baby brother. And she loved that baby brother and fussed over him and soothed him when he cried and made him laugh when he was lonely. Only then a terrible thing happened. The little prince died."

Cassandra warns me with her eyes.

"People said it was an accident, a terrible accident. And the princess thought of the lad who'd left her and the little brother she couldn't save, and she felt . . . helpless. Foolish. Powerless. And she hated that feeling more than anything.

"So she decided, Screw this. I'm not going to be a princess any-more. Princesses can't do squat. I will be a witch. Because witches have power. I will punish and destroy, as proof of my great power. I will be stronger and smarter than everyone."

Cassandra smiles brokenly. "I was always bummed when the witch died."

Then the smile dissolves, and all of Cassandra with it. Her

breath comes in short, shallow waves as she gasps, "The very last thing he heard was me screaming at him. He must have been . . . so . . . scared."

She starts sobbing. I slide my arms under hers, take her head on my shoulder. The waves of misery pound on my neck, her bristly wet eyelashes, the hot slick of tears on her face. Finally, the crying quiets. Cassandra sits back. She sits like a child, legs folded under her, head drooping, staring down at her knees.

"I want him back so bad," she whispers.

"I know."

"But I can't make that happen, can I?"

"No."

"I just—I just wanted to hear my own head, you know? That's why I put on those earphones. Turned the volume way up. And all the time—"

She shakes her head sharply, refusing to cry again. She sniffles loudly, says, "I should die too. If we're talking what I deserve."

"I would not say that."

"I would." She looks at me. "If someone else did this to Eamonn? I'd want to kill them."

I know that this is true. I don't know how to make Cassandra not feel it. She is the prince who saves and the evil queen.

"Witches aren't real, Cassandra," I say. "Stupid is real. Selfish is real."

"Cruelty," she says.

"Yeah. And dying is easy. You know that." I look pointedly at her wrists.

She looks too. "Yeah, the thing with the pretty boy? I had decided he was going to be my real life. That I'd move in with him, and we'd take Eamonn out to the park, have him over. But I'd have one place that was mine."

"Then Pretty Boy left and no more escape."

"Yeah, except for this." She frowns at her wrist. "Screwed that up."

Cassandra breathes in, then exhales. "What the fuck am I going to tell my parents?"

That they asked too much? That it was all too much? And you all have to figure out how to deal with that?

"You're cool with words, Cassandra," I say. "You'll figure it out."

Cassandra stands up, brushes the dirt and twigs from her jacket. "It'd be awesome, wouldn't it? If magic were real and you could bring people back to life."

"Yeah."

"So now what?"

I think of the kisses, the laughter in the cafeteria. All those people clustered around Ella, wanting to show her they can heal, not hurt. I think of Isabelle, the way she was so scared to stand up for me, but how she did it anyway. I think of the pain you feel when you do the wrong thing—and you can never take it back.

"Like you said," I tell her. "Use your power wisely."

I hold out my hand. Cassandra takes it. Her sleeve rides up as she does and I see the faint scars on her wrist. I turn my hand a little, to show my scar. Cassandra winces and smiles at the same time.

As we navigate our way down the rocky slope, she says, "Scary."

"Yeah. Go slow."

I squeeze her hand and we go together.

ABOUT THE AUTHOR

Mariah Fredericks was born and raised in New York City. She is the author of *The Girl in the Park,* which *Publishers Weekly,* in a starred review, called "profound, provocative commentary on what it means to grow up in the age of Facebook." Mariah's other books include the bestseller *The True Meaning of Cleavage,* as well as *Head Games, Crunch Time,* and the In the Cards series. Visit her at mariahfredericks.com.